Praise for *Hiroshima Boy*

"I've always admired Naomi Hirahara's Mas Arai. A brilliant, unique addition to mystery fiction from the very beginning, his character has straddled time, place, and culture, with roots in one of the most terrible acts of violence war has ever inflicted upon humanity. And Mas has prevailed while growing older in a country that does not always value the wisdom of its elders, or those who work with their hands. This may be the last entry in the series (really?), but I am sure readers will come to love Mas for years—he is one of a kind. *Hiroshima Boy* is a wonderful finale to a fine mystery series. Kudos to Naomi Hirahara."

> — Jacqueline Winspear, author of the *New York Times*–bestselling Maisie Dobbs mysteries

"With *Hiroshima Boy*, Naomi Hirahara offers readers another fine, artfully understated story about a man who believes himself to be average, yet is anything but. Carrying the ashes of his deceased best friend, Mas Arai returns to Hiroshima, where he spent his childhood and was witness to the bomb that devastated the city and its populace. When Mas stumbles onto the body of a murdered boy, what began as a simple mission to keep a recent promise becomes a complex journey in understanding the past. Like a Zen poet, Hirahara creates a quiet surface with a powerful storm beneath. The novel purports to be the last in this Edgar Award–winning series. We can only hope that Naomi Hirahara has a change of heart."

> — William Kent Krueger, *New York Times*–bestselling author of *Ordinary Grace* and the Cork O'Connor mysteries

Praise for the Mas Arai Mysteries

"A shrewd sense of character and a formidable narrative engine."
— *Chicago Tribune*

"Hirahara's well-plotted, wholesome whodunit offers a unique look at LA's Japanese American community, with enough twists and local flavor to keep you guessing till the end."
— *Entertainment Weekly*

"In a genre in which unusual amateur sleuths are the norm, Mas Arai is in a class by himself."
— Oline Cogdill, *Florida Sun-Sentinel*

"This perfectly balanced gem deserves a wide readership."
— *Publishers Weekly*

"In author Hirahara's deft hands (she's an Edgar winner), the human characters, especially Mas, always make for a compelling read."
— *Mystery Scene*

"Hirahara has a keen eye for the telling detail and an assured sense of character."
— *Los Angeles Times*

"Mas is a hyperobservant, methodical sleuth—a blend of Columbo and Hercule Poirot—but what makes this award-winning series shine is the way Hirahara takes readers inside her character's head. A winner."

— *Booklist*

"A thoughtful and highly entertaining read."

— *Library Journal* (starred review)

"The series is one of my favorites, and though Mas's circumstances change with each installation, the books all stand alone, on the shoulders of one gruff, aging Japanese American gardener and Hiroshima survivor with an unfortunate tendency to wander into complex murder mysteries."

— *Los Angeles Review of Books*

"Hirahara's complex and compassionate portrait of a contemporary American subculture enhances her mystery, and vice versa."

— *Kirkus Reviews*

"What makes this series unique is its flawed and honorable protagonist.... A fascinating insight into a complex and admirable man."

— *Booklist* (starred review)

Hiroshima Boy

Naomi Hirahara

PROSPECT
·PARK·
BOOKS

Published by Prospect Park Books
2359 Lincoln Avenue
Altadena, California 91001
www.prospectparkbooks.com

PROSPECT
· PARK ·
BOOKS

Distributed by Consortium Book Sales & Distribution
www.cbsd.com

Library of Congress Cataloging-in-Publication Data
Names: Hirahara, Naomi, 1962- author.
Title: Hiroshima boy : a Mas Arai mystery / Naomi Hirahara.
Description: Altadena, California : Prospect Park Books, [2018] |
Series: Mas Arai series ; 7
Identifiers: LCCN 2017040325 (print) | LCCN 2017042432 (ebook) |
ISBN 9781945551093 (Ebook) | ISBN 9781945551086 (paperback)
Subjects: LCSH: Murder—Investigation—Fiction. |
GSAFD: Mystery fiction.
Classification: LCC PS3608.I76 (ebook) | LCC PS3608.I76 H57 2018
(print) | DDC 813/.6--dc23
LC record available at https://lccn.loc.gov/2017040325

Design by Amy Inouye, Future Studio

Printed in the United States of America

TO THE *HIBAKUSHA*

More Mas Arai Mysteries

Sayonara Slam
Strawberry Yellow
Blood Hina
Snakeskin Shamisen
Gasa-Gasa Girl
Summer of the Big Bachi

More Fiction by Naomi Hirahara

Grave on Grand Avenue (an Officer Ellie Rush mystery)
Murder on Bamboo Lane (an Officer Ellie Rush mystery)
1001 Cranes

Selected Nonfiction by Naomi Hirahara

A Scent of Flowers:
The History of the Southern California Flower Market

An American Son:
The Story of George Aratani,
Founder of Mikasa and Kenwood

Green Makers:
Japanese American Gardeners in Southern California

Life after Manzanar (cowritten with Heather Lindquist)

Terminal Island: Lost Communities of Los Angeles Harbor
(cowritten with Geraldine Knatz)

Chapter One

Mas Arai was worried that the customs officer at Kansai Airport would find his best friend, Haruo Mukai, inside his suitcase. Mas had wrapped him in an old plastic bag, tied the top with green gardening twine, and stuffed the package in one of his worn socks. If Mas's wife, Genessee, had not been in a convalescent home, recovering from knee surgery, everything would have transpired so differently. For one, he would have had a proper suitcase, not one with a broken roller wheel. And two, she would have consulted the authorities with the airlines to discover the proper way to transport ashes of a dead man. But all that was *mendokusai* for Mas. A hassle. An inconvenience. If you need to get from point A to point B, you just draw a straight line, he thought. Talking always wasted time.

He had been remarried for six years. Remarkable for an old retired gardener who was now pushing eighty-six. Love had sucker punched him, blinded him when he wasn't looking or expecting it. His marriage to his first wife, Chizuko, made much more sense. He was a thirtysomething bachelor in Los Angeles and it was time. His family in Hiroshima suggested that he return to Japan to get a wife, which he did. That was the last time he'd stepped foot in Japan. That is, until now.

Back then there had been no airport here in Kansai, about 250 miles from the area where he'd spent his youth. He was no expert on airplanes or airports, but this one looked similar to LAX, at least behind the scenes. Sure, here the officers were all Japanese men and women, some wearing white masks to prevent the spread of their sick germs, but they had the same steely stare. Looks that could strip him down in an instant. Whether it was in the US or Japan, uniformed officers knew that he didn't quite belong.

The man in front of him had a big black mole on one cheek. Mas wondered if the officer had had it as a child and whether it was always the same size or had grown as he aged. If it was the former, he must have endured much bullying.

"Are you American?" the officer asked in English, as if the blue passport cover was a fraud.

"Yes," Mas answered back in Japanese.

The officer's gaze remained on Mas. Mas, on the other hand, could not take his eyes off the giant mole.

"Fine." The man gestured that he could proceed.

He had made it through.

Mas had heard that Kansai Airport had been built on

a man-made island. Just the thought of that made him feel a bit queasy, as if he couldn't depend on the integrity of the land.

In terms of land transportation, he attempted to read the instructions from Genessee, who had looked up all the information on her cell phone from her hospital bed and had even written it down. The only problem was that he could barely read her handwriting, which was loopy and imprecise. Chizuko's, on the other hand, had been picture perfect from a missionary's instruction in Hiroshima. She brought that perfection with her to America.

His and Chizuko's only child, Mari, had also tried to help by showing him train and bus schedules and sightseeing stops on her laptop. Of course, he had retained nothing and had even forgotten her printouts on his kitchen table. This trip was not about seeing the sights anyway. It was about wham, bam, getting things done. All he knew was that he was to meet someone at Hiroshima Station later that afternoon.

Seeing the blue sky through the wall of windows, Mas instinctively headed outside. The minute he left the artificially cooled airport, he was hit with a wall of heat. He had noted on an airport clock earlier that it was eight o'clock in the morning in Japan, and the humidity pressed down on his face, entering his ear canals, nostrils, and throat. The tail end of July, he'd heard, was the absolute worst time to travel in Japan, and, of course, Haruo had to die in the summer. Even in his death, Haruo wasn't doing Mas any favors. And Mas knew that if he waited until fall, he himself might not be alive, not to mention Haruo's older sister, the recipient of the ashes.

There were some buses lined up in a row and he figured he would head south. The bus driver attempted to take the broken suitcase and place it in the bottom storage unit, but Mas didn't want to be separated from it. He wrestled it away and took it into the bus. It careened into the knees of irritated passengers as it bounced behind him through the narrow middle aisle. He finally found an open spot and stuffed it into an overhead shelf.

He swore as he settled in his seat. And to the suitcase above, he said silently, *Haruo, see. Youzu make me come all the way ova here.*

This trip was the most *mendokusai* thing that he had ever done in his life, other than perhaps flying to pick up Chizuko from Hiroshima. Somewhere in his garage was a remnant of that inconvenient trip, a Pan Am flight bag covered with decades of dust, sticky grime, and even droppings from a mouse that had certainly lost its way.

"Excuse me, excuse," someone was speaking to him in Japanese.

Mas blinked hard and tried to remember where he was. The bus felt different. It was plusher than the hard seats of the Metro back in Los Angeles. The driver had taken down his suitcase and placed it in the aisle. *Why couldn't he keep his hands off of my private property?*

He almost stumbled down the stairs to the curb and gazed up to see a white, modern building that resembled a giant humidifier. "Where are you going?" the driver asked him. Mas took out his wife's illegible notes, and the driver directed him inside. The suitcase bumping sideways behind him, he made his way down the platform and into the modest station. There was a wall of ticket machines with grids of some cities that he hadn't heard of. What had happened during the more than fifty years that he had been away?

Passersby ignored him, probably assuming that he knew where he was going. He looked a hundred percent Japanese, after all. He finally approached a window next to the rows of ticket gates. A young man in a black railway hat and blue uniform appeared in the window, holding some kind of metal tool in his right hand.

"Ah, I'm going to Hiroshima," Mas managed to say in Japanese.

"You can get your ticket from the machines there. Or go to the Green Window."

Green Window? What the hell was a Green Window?

Just then a group of five teenagers pressed behind him, holding up some kind of pass in their wallets. He stepped aside with his broken suitcase, feeling more lost than he ever did in America. Even though there were rules in the US, there always seem to be rule breakers. People looked different and acted differently from each other. Here, people seemed to be programmed similarly. Sure there was the random Japanese bohemian with dreadlocks carrying a surfboard, but he moved in concert with the flow of Japan.

Mas, on the other hand, was a knot in the middle of the smooth silk string, the scratch on the vinyl record. Even though he had lived in Japan from age three to eighteen, his birthplace, America, where he spent the past almost seventy years, had made him a stranger here.

He wandered in a circle, hoping to seize upon anything that could direct him to where he needed to go. And then he saw it. A sign with the Japanese writing, *Midori no Madoguchi*. Literally Green Window. And then an arrow.

It turned out there were no green windows in this ticket office, just a green image of a stick figure sitting back in a reclined seat. But there were workers—again not wearing anything green—who seemed to be solving problems and issuing tickets to a line of people. Waiting in the line was a *hakujin*, a white man with unruly hair, a smelly backpack at his side. This could have been his own son-in-law, Lloyd, maybe twenty-five years ago. If the Green Window people could help the backpacker, they could surely help him.

Once he finally reached the counter, the clerk didn't bother to look at his face and seemed unfazed by his rough-and-tumble Japanese. She obviously had dealt with a wide range of gaijin travelers and had no expectations of him. For a few glorious minutes, Mas felt free to be himself—an ignorant outsider who was not being judged. Then an envelope with the ticket was placed in his hand, and he was released to the wilds beyond the Green Window.

Even trying to find the correct place to stand on the platform was a challenge. There seemed to be random numbers and he couldn't quite find where he needed to be. He felt embarrassed to approach the *hakujin* backpacker, but it would be worse to bother the slick salarymen and polished office ladies who were focused on their newspapers or cell phones.

"Ah, I stand here?" He asked lifting his ticket to the man's eye level.

The backpacker seemed flattered to be approached by an old Japanese man. "This is for assigned seats," he replied in an accent that wasn't American. "You should stand there." He pointed to a row on one end of the platform.

Truth be told, Mas was curious about riding in a bullet train. High-speed rail had come after he and Chizuko had gotten married. Would it indeed shoot forward as fast as a projectile from a gun? Although he was not one to get carsick, he braced himself for a new experience. First a fake island and now a train traveling two hundred miles per hour.

Just then the train arrived, its front shaped like a dolphin's nose. Everything about the bullet train was sleek and silent. Mas stepped forward, almost bumping into the old woman standing in front of him, but no one moved. A line of women in pink uniforms rushed in with rag bags and turned the seats around, wiping them down and replacing doilies on the headrests with new ones.

He was transfixed with how the cleaners worked with such purpose. In a few minutes they were finished and appeared at the entrance of the trains with smiles on their faces. The train was now ready for its passengers to make their way down the spine of the archipelago.

The train was not crowded, and he opted for a window seat. Again, he pushed the suitcase with Haruo's ashes up into an overhead shelf. Luckily, it was low, not like the high shelves in America.

Sitting down, he glanced at his Casio watch, which was nowhere close to the correct time in Japan. Most people, he noticed, had already ordered a lunch box before entering the bullet train. They placed their elegant purchases on the pull-down tray in front of their seats. Even though these bentos were the Japanese equivalent of American takeout food, at least monetarily and conveniencewise, they were nothing like the greasy and messy paper sleeves holding hamburgers and fries, his go-to food back in Southern California.

No, instead these containers were filled with marinated carrots cut like maple leaves, rice balls formed in perfect triangles and dressed in spiffy suits of nori, and beautifully grilled and glazed pieces of fish.

Mas's mouth watered. He, of course, had eaten in the airplane, better food than he had anticipated. Everything was wrapped and had its own compartment or container. Even the water came in a bag that you could pour into a plastic cup.

Usually such organization eluded and frustrated him, but as soon as he left LAX to travel across the Pacific, he felt something happen to him—like a cord had been pulled, freeing the defensiveness he had felt all those years that he lived in the US. California was his home, his birthplace. But in some places, even on his customers' lawns, he had to be on guard. He belonged, yet he didn't belong. Perhaps he would feel differently in Japan?

A female worker pushed a cart filled with box lunches, drinks, and souvenirs. Mas chose a small one with three rice balls, each one flavored a little distinctly. If anything could clear his head, it would be rice with the sour tang of pickled plum.

He also ordered a Coke, and was amused to be handed a can much skinnier than he was used to. He could completely wrap his fingers around this one—and when he was in the height of his gardening days, could probably have finished it off in one gulp.

For a moment he thought about buying a toy train for his only grandson, Takeo. But Takeo wasn't a child anymore. He was in high school, not interested in anything that didn't have a screen for digital images.

As the train zoomed forward, he heard only a low-volume whooshing sound against the window. The familiar scenes of rice paddies and farmhouses outside calmed him to no end. This was the Japan he remembered. The Japan that time had forgotten.

For a moment, he wished that Haruo wasn't stuffed in his suitcase but was fully alive, next to him, watching this scene. Haruo had gone back to Japan a couple of times with his daughter, but as far as Mas knew he'd had no strong desire to be buried here.

The request—or perhaps edict—came from Haruo's

older sister, Ayako. This sister, *nesan*, whom he had only heard of once in passing. Like Haruo, she'd been born in Fresno and taken to Hiroshima as a child. Unlike Haruo, she stayed in Japan. He wasn't sure why, because he understood that she'd never married. And she was ancient, almost ninety, but had had enough energy to call Haruo's widow, Spoon, every day.

Spoon, who was so hunched over now that she resembled a round piece of fruit, could barely sustain such persistent calls. Also, Ayako didn't seem to either recognize or honor that there was an international time difference that separated Hiroshima and Los Angeles by sixteen, seventeen hours. As a result, Spoon received these calls at two o'clock every morning.

Spoon wasn't able to make the international trip. And it wasn't like she could put Haruo in an envelope or old coffee can and send him off to Hiroshima. The task had to be in person, and as it turned out, Mas was the best and maybe the only available person for the job.

He, quite honestly, thought the whole idea was ridiculous. If it were him, he would have preferred to be blown in the California wind, scattered in the weeds, grass, and flowers, and end up on a sparrow's wing, unnoticed and without any fanfare.

She was holding a handwritten sign with his name in purple, "MASAO ARAI." And below it, in Japanese. The Japanese was all in katakana, the script used for foreign names, not Japanese ones. Even the writing itself looked babyish, written by an outsider. The girl holding the sign was, in fact, an outsider. Her skin was dark, copper toned, and her eyes seemed too large for her head. Young men would deem her attractive, but to Mas, she seemed skinny and delicate. A child.

The lopsided suitcase behind him, Mas stood in front of the girl on the platform. In spite of her youth, she looked weary. She must have been waiting a long time.

"Are you Arai-*san*?" she asked.

He grunted. Haruo's sister had indicated that she would send someone to pick him up from Hiroshima Station, but he didn't imagine anyone who looked like this.

As he took a few more steps, it dawned on him. It was here. Not in this actual building, but in this physical space. This is where he had been. The bursting of atoms and molecules, the obliteration of the train station and the fire.

"Are you all right? *Daijobu?*"

He was doubled over his bag, and the girl helped him to his feet. Making sure that he was steady, she ran over to the vending machine next to the snack stand and got him a cold bottle of water.

The water was actually exactly what he needed. He felt immediately revived.

"Do you feel more comfortable speaking English or Japanese?"

He didn't quite know how to answer that question. He didn't enjoy speaking at all, especially as he grew older.

The words didn't come to either his mind or mouth that easily these days.

"My name is Thea." Anticipating any questions he might have, she added, "I'm from the Philippines."

Most of the signs in the airport and train platforms were not only in English, but also in Chinese and Korean. Something had happened to the town he had grown up in—the same thing that had happened in America. The world had entered in.

"You've had such a long trip. You must be very tired."

At least the girl had a semblance of common sense.

"Youzu how ole?" Mas finally said.

"Me?" Her face flushed slightly. She must get that question often. "Twenty. Mukai-*sensei* is my sponsor. She was my mother's nursing professor."

"Your mama here?"

Thea shook her head. "She is back in the Philippines. But she loved Japan, especially Hiroshima, so much. She told me that if I had the opportunity, I should come to Hiroshima, too." She took the half-empty water bottle from him and tightened the cap before stuffing it in her canvas bag next to her "MASAO ARAI" sign. "Do you feel strong enough to continue?"

He nodded, grabbing hold of the suitcase's retractable handle.

"I want to take you straight to the island."

They got into a taxi with Thea telling the driver in perfect Japanese that they wanted to go to Ujina Port. From there, Mas guessed, they would take a ferry to Ino Island.

Ayako Mukai lived in a nursing home on Ino. As a child, Mas had gone to the island to go hiking. Ino was called the Little Mount Fuji of Hiroshima. Aside from being the approximate sloped shape, the mountain was, of course, nothing like Mount Fuji. The thing that had impressed him the most was Ino's chorus of *semi,* cicada, which buzzed and screeched louder than anything he'd ever heard as a boy. The sound was so penetrating that it hurt his then-young developing ribs.

But after the Bomb fell, Ino's legacy had been forever altered. Mas didn't hear about the details until days later, when he had finally returned to his home from the middle of Hiroshima. The makeshift rafts, the lifeboats that people rode to escape the flattened and burning city, the black rain. Ino, which had once quarantined soldiers who'd been exposed to cholera, still had its buildings intact. There were places for ruined bodies to rest on the floor underneath a roof to shield them from the punishing heat. Ten thousand people had come to Ino seeking refuge. Unfortunately, far, far fewer were able to leave the island alive.

He wasn't that interested in revisiting the island, especially during the height of summer. Why would Ayako Mukai want to spend her last years, months, and days in a place marked by the *pikadon,* the blast of the atomic bomb? The anguished cries of his classmates had followed him to the other side of the Pacific Ocean, tormenting him in the middle of the night. He couldn't imagine living in the midst of those ghosts today.

Reaching Ujina, they waited in a quiet port building, which was mostly empty. It looked relatively new, with high ceilings and a wall of glass that faced the ocean. In the distance was Ino, a mound of green. After waiting about half an hour, they walked outside to the landing, where about five or six young boys, little *yogore* troublemaker types, were running around causing mischief. A couple threw rocks into the water, while the others laughed and tossed a baseball cap, apparently the smallest boy's, to one another. Americans had the impression that Asian children were well behaved, but they had not been exposed to these unsupervised boys, who actually could have been Mas and his friends, once upon a time.

Their ferry appeared on the horizon, becoming larger and larger. It was at least a two-decker with a parking area for cars. "The last boat from Ino to Ujina is at eight in the evening," Thea said. "If you don't make that one, you're stuck on the island overnight." Not a great prospect, since there was only one inn on Ino, she explained.

The boys had run ahead to the ticket taker, who had walked down to the landing from the boat. Thea and Mas were last to board and before he could take out any yen that he had exchanged in Los Angeles before he departed, Thea handed two large coins to the ticket collector. The coins went into his leather satchel, which looked like an American woman's old-fashioned pocketbook. Mas made a move to pay Thea back, but she shook her head and laughed.

"Please. Mukai-*sensei* has taken care of everything."

They climbed up a flight of stairs into an enclosed passenger area, rows of seats divided into three sections.

"I get a bit seasick, even on such a short trip like this. I'll be outside. But please rest your feet." Thea walked up one of the aisles through the door to a small deck. As the ferry began to move forward, her long, dark brown hair whipped behind her, evoking the image of a young pony overlooking a wide expanse of land.

He propped his legs across three seats in the back row. He realized that this was a very un-Japanese thing for an old man to be doing, but he didn't care. This trip, which had just started, had already been rough on his battered body. He had a couple of hard candies in his jeans pocket and took them out, in addition to an old slim camera that Mari had given to him. He imagined Mari nagging him, *Dad, take some pictures while you're there. You haven't been there in almost fifty years.* To silence her, he pressed the shutter a good three, four times, not even paying attention to what he was photographing. *There, good enough?* he thought.

The main passenger area was relatively empty, aside from two rows of the rowdy teenage boys. They were still harassing the little one, who still didn't have his baseball cap. Across the aisle from these boys was another one, maybe fourteen years old, who sat by himself. Mas noticed him for two reasons. First of all, his face was downcast, as if he were upset or stressed. Perhaps the boys had done something to him, too? Had he been ousted from the group for some reason? The other thing that made the boy stand out was his

T-shirt. It was bright red with a cable car on its back. When he abruptly stood up and turned, the words "San Francisco" on the front of the shirt caught Mas's eye.

When he was nineteen, Mas had spent some time in San Francisco after working the strawberry fields in Watsonville. He lived in the home of a rich *hakujin* man, for whom he worked as a schoolboy, a term that Japanese Americans used for houseboy. It was a short-lived experiment. He was summarily fired when his benefactor discovered that friends and cousins had spent the night on the floor in his tiny servant's quarters.

He did not regret that he had lost his schoolboy position. He wasn't meant to answer to one boss. And San Francisco, with its colorful Fisherman's Wharf, sourdough bread, and cable cars, was meant to be experienced to its fullest, at least until the money ran out.

He doubted that this brooding teen had spent any length of time in San Francisco. America was definitely not for the weak.

A car was waiting for them when they arrived in Ino. This was the main dock on the island, Thea said. A smaller landing on the east side was closer to the nursing home, but the big car ferry couldn't dock there, the girl explained.

The boys ran off the boat, scattering like crabs into the narrow alleys of the small seaside village. Mas was relieved for the quiet. The sun again seemed to burn through his clothing and he wished he'd brought his Dodgers cap to at least shield his eyes. A concrete *toro* gateway welcomed them to the island. Behind it was a simple shrine with a peaked roof covered in green patina, probably from saltwater exposure.

The driver of the car, Tatsuo, worked at the nursing home. Of an indeterminate age, he wore a loose white cotton uniform and awkward sandals on his stockinged feet. After placing the suitcase into the trunk, Tatsuo made sure his passengers were secured in their seats before driving forward. The narrow, winding highway could barely accommodate two cars going in opposite directions. Luckily, there weren't many vehicles to avoid, only an occasional motorbike or bicycle.

They passed the only inn on the island, a modest *ryokan* that looked like the type that offerered meals of fresh fish and local vegetables. The driver made a left at what seemed the southernmost tip, the site of an expansive garden lined with sunflowers and dahlias, across from a large building that could have been a school.

The ocean was at low tide, revealing rows of racks holding oyster spats. When he was a boy in Hiroshima, Mas had assisted an uncle in threading large white scallop shells with rope. He wasn't quite sure how it worked, but somehow the baby oysters attached to the smooth inside surface of the shells.

"We don't eat oysters right now, though. It's off-season. I've heard that in the summer a bacteria can be spread to the oysters as they spawn." Thea then repeated what she said in

Japanese to Tatsuo and he nodded.

"Only certain kinds of oysters, though," he said in Japanese. "We have all kinds now."

Mas wasn't aware of the seasonal ban. He was a bit disappointed because he was looking forward to eating one of Hiroshima's specialties, *kaki furai*, or fried oysters.

"Tatsuo-*san* knows all about oysters. His uncle even has a factory here," Thea reported.

The car finally stopped in front of a two-story institutional-looking building.

Mas was always a bit scared to go into any kind of nursing home. His biggest fear was to spend his last days trapped in one of these facilities. This one, though, seemed better than most. At least the ocean was a stone's throw away.

Leaving their shoes at the *genkan*, the recessed Japanese entryway, Thea helped him into oversized slippers made from some kind of synthetic material that was neither plastic nor nylon.

"Let's say hi to Mukai-*sensei*," Thea said, taking hold of his suitcase. "She's usually in bed by seven o'clock."

He again felt his stomach flip-flop. He didn't know much about Haruo's sister. Haruo had mentioned some brothers in Hiroshima and maybe Ayako in passing once. Or maybe Haruo did talk about his sister when Mas wasn't listening, which was actually quite often.

After being cleared to pass through a security door, they traveled down a wide corridor.

"Your suitcase wheel is broken," Thea announced, a bit irritated with its awkward roll.

What else was new?

Finally they stopped in front of an open doorway. "Mukai-*sensei*—" Thea called out to someone lying in a hospital bed. "*Ojama shimasu*, pardon me for disturbing you." She and Mas both bowed before entering the room. On one side was a private bathroom.

"So you are Mas Arai."

At first he couldn't make out the speaker's features because of the sunlight through a picture window overlooking the ocean.

As his failing eyes acclimated to the light, he almost audibly gasped. The sister resembled Haruo so much—sans the ugly keloid scar that had marked the left side of his face.

"I am Ayako," she said in English. Her voice had almost a regal tone.

He bowed again.

"Where is he?"

Mas realized that Ayako meant her brother. But how could he open up his suitcase to reveal his worn (but clean, of course) underwear bunched up next to the sock holding Haruo's ashes? It was the ultimate embarrassment, a *haji* that he was loath to experience.

"Perhaps Arai-*san* can rest first. He's had such a long day of travel." Mas was grateful that Thea saved him.

"We have an extra room for guests here. I hope you can handle sleeping on a futon on the floor."

What kind of Japanese did Ayako think he was?

"We will speak more later. Thea, show him where his room is."

Mas felt like he was being officially dismissed—from what? This was not a queen's castle but a modest room in a nursing home on a remote island.

In the hallway, Thea whispered, "She's a bit frightening. I've gotten used to her."

At least Ayako's pompousness was not a figment of his imagination. He followed Thea to the guest room, which was a six-tatami-mat room, about a hundred square feet, with a sink behind a sliding door.

After helping him with his suitcase, she asked, "Is there anything more I can get for you?"

"Needsu to make phone call. My wife."

"Oh, I thought that—never mind, of course. You can use my cell phone."

Mas resisted. That was too much of an imposition.

"Okay, here, come to the office with me."

They returned to the lobby and entered the front office through a side door. Thea spoke briefly to Tatsuo, and Mas was brought over to a back room. After getting his home number, Thea dialed for him and handed him the receiver. A few strange rings and then it was his blessed wife on the line.

"Hello."

"Hallo."

"Mas, you made it. Thank God. Mari and I have been so worried. Where are you?"

"Ino Island."

"You must be exhausted."

He grunted.

"So you saw Haruo's sister? She must have been so appreciative that you came all the way with his ashes."

He didn't mention anything about Haruo being smashed in his sock. "Yah," he just managed to say.

He kept his conversation with Genessee brief. These international calls were expensive, and his intent was to let her know that he was still alive.

"Oh, by the way," she interjected, "Mari wanted me to tell you that your niece has been calling her. She wants to know whether you'll be visiting your family's house."

"Umm," was all Mas said. He didn't want to think about that now. He had a task to do. This was not about fun and games and going back home. Besides there was no one left in that home—at least no people that he knew.

After he finished his call, Thea was already sitting on the *genkan*, her shoes back on her feet.

"I have to go back to my apartment.... I'll try to check in every day you are here," she said.

As she rose, Mas was surprised that he wasn't relieved. He wanted her to stay and be his advocate. There were too many unknowns on the island, a beautiful but somewhat brutal place.

"Oh, by the way," Thea added, "there are sundowners here. So make sure you lock your door at night from the inside. The men's bathroom is across from your room. Make sure to lock it, too, when you use it. They won't hurt you, of course, but they might be a bit confused."

He himself was a bit confused, and Thea, picking up on it, elaborated. "Sundowners are seniors who get a bit agitated when the sun goes down. Who knows why it happens? A bit like vampires, *desho?*"

Thea's comment on the elderly vampires shook Mas a little. As soon as he locked himself in his room, he turned on the television. It was a modern flat screen but on the smallish side. There were only about seven channels available, and he chose a comedy show that featured strange-looking Japanese people spouting nonsense from a puffy couch. The comedians were ridiculous, but the audience laughter comforted him.

Zipping open his suitcase, he pulled out his pajamas and gazed at the sock stuffed with the plastic bag with Haruo's ashes. Haruo needed to be released from the old, faded sock. He placed the bag next to a vase holding a yellow silk rose on a low table by the television set.

That night, on the tatami floor, he found it difficult to sleep. It may have been jet lag—what time was it in California? He turned on the light and checked his watch. Eight a.m. in Los Angeles. He had reached his destination, so he should finally be able to relax. But in his gut he felt that something was not right.

His tiny room had a sink, and he went to it to splash water on his face. Thea had left the water bottle she'd purchased for him by the sink, and he finished it off. He didn't realize how dehydrated he was. He returned to the futon and may have slept for a few minutes, but then he opened his eyes. Now he needed to go to the restroom.

He undid the lock on the door and looked both ways in the hallway. A dim light on one end revealed nothing but the large open corridor. He'd forgotten his slippers in his room, and the linoleum floor felt cold against his bare soles. He quickly went into the bathroom, fastened the bolt on the door, and did his business. Maybe now sleep could come.

The hallway was empty when he reentered his room. As he turned to slide close his door and lock it, he heard a rustling near his futon.

An old woman, her hair in disarray, stood on the other side of the tatami mat. She was wearing a *chanchanko*, a Japanese padded vest. For a moment, he thought her eyes were missing but then realized that her sockets were sunken in and obscured by loose flesh.

"Be careful. It's dangerous," she said. "Don't believe what they say."

Mas was so shocked he didn't know how to respond. There were alarms in the hallway to alert the staff. He took a few steps back and went out to the hallway to find the best way to call for help. But by the time he reached the alarm, he saw the woman leave his room and head for the other side of the hallway.

"*Baka*," he cursed at the disappearing woman. *Stupid*. She'd shaken him, but obviously she was harmless. He decided not to call anyone in the middle of the night. If he couldn't deal with a half-witted old resident, his days as an independent man were numbered.

Hampered by interrupted sleep, he was severely annoyed to be awakened by the intense light from the morning sun. The curtains were opaque, and there was no way to reduce the sunlight. *Shikataganai*, he thought—nothing can be done about it. His watch read twelve noon, so it was probably only four in the morning here in Hiroshima. He could not go back to sleep, so he decided to wander around outside.

In the lobby he traded his slippers for his shoes and waved at the worker behind the desk to open the glass doors. He walked up the concrete road, past small oyster-production factories covered in corrugated aluminum. Their operations seemed shuttered for the summer months. Stacks of threaded white scallop shells, resembling giant puka shell necklaces like the ones Mari wore in high school, were placed in piles on their sides. Plastic tubes that probably were used to connect the shells were packed upright in crates.

He had seen at least one man fishing from a cement platform and wondered what kind of fish could be caught in these waters. He himself was a surf fisherman—at least in his prime—and he loved the pull of the rod in his hands, the constant fight with the caught fish, a dance of release and then a quick reeling in.

Surprisingly, the surf did not smell as salty as the times he fished the Pacific Ocean from the shores of California. Instead of a polluted brown, the water had a greenish tint.

He looked toward a makeshift jetty, which housed a small boat with a motor. What was that floating in the water beside it?

A red flag? But it seemed attached to something. A knot of seaweed, perhaps? Curious, he walked down to the platform, made of gigantic bamboo poles, now weathered gray, that had been tied together with wire to planks of wood.

The way the red item bobbed in the water was suspect. It certainly was not from the sea. As he got closer, he almost lost his breath. He could make out a head of black hair about two inches underwater. He should have immediately gone for help, but the floating body was calling out to him.

He broke loose a deteriorating bamboo pole from the jetty and pulled the body toward him. As the body turned in the water, the face, bloated and fleshy, came to the surface. The eyes were closed, but the mouth was open. A small dark fish darted in and out from the lips. The red that Mas had seen from the hill above had been a T-shirt that the floating body was wearing—with "San Francisco" emblazoned across its chest.

Chapter Two

The sun continued to beat down on the asphalt road. Mas wanted to run, but he forced himself to take measured, steady steps. He thought he saw a cut rope on the concrete, but it was a huge, thick worm, searching for an escape from the heat.

"There's a boy out there in the ocean," he told Tatsuo behind the desk in Japanese. "He's dead."

"Dead?" Tatsuo sprang into action. He called another employee, and they rushed from the office into the lobby. Sliding into sandals lined up at the *genkan*, they ran outside. Mas followed and watched as they headed down the slope toward the rickety jetty.

A small crowd had formed along the hill overlooking the water. News spread quickly on this island, even a little after sunrise.

"I think it's a boy," someone said.

"Is he from the Children's Home?"

A man who looked as if he could be in his thirties shook his head. He had thick, pitch-black hair and the beginning of a goatee. "All our children are accounted for. He's not one of ours."

None of the villagers claimed him as one of theirs, either. It was too hard to see the body from this position, anyway.

Mas heard the zoom of a motorbike, and then saw it stop on the side of the road. The rider removed his helmet, revealing short-cropped graying hair and wire-rimmed sunglasses.

"Ah, Gohata-*san* has arrived," the man from the Children's Home commented dryly. By the tone of his voice, Mas knew that this Gohata was not well thought of, at least by this man, who was presumably the head of the home.

"What happened?" Gohata asked, adjusting his sunglasses. He was wearing a heavy silver ring set with an opal stone.

Then a chorus of villagers.

"It's a boy."

"He's dead."

"This one discovered him." One of them gestured toward Mas.

"Who are you?" Gohata asked.

"Arai. Arai Mas." Surnames were always said first in Japan. The family name was more important than any name made up at birth.

"Gohata Bunpei. I am the district representative here." He looked Mas up and down. "Are you Japanese?" he asked with all condescension possible.

"He's Mukai-*san*'s guest. From America," the same

villager said. Mas was surprised to hear that so much was known about his situation. After all, he was a complete stranger and had not met any of them before.

"Shouldn't someone call the police?" Mas asked in Japanese.

"No police here," the villager said.

Gohata glared at Mas, perhaps annoyed that his authority was considered inadequate in this situation. He took out his cell phone from his shirt pocket and went to the side of the road to make his call.

"Arai-*san*, I am Ikeda Toshi. Nice to meet you." The man from the Children's Home took this opportunity to introduce himself. He was about a head taller than Mas, and his eyebrows were as dark as his hair. Mas bowed back in response.

"Sorry about Gohata. He thinks that he runs the place," Toshi said.

"He does run the place," one of the villagers said.

"But he's not even originally from Ino," another chimed in. "He's an Okayama man who married an Ino woman."

"But I guess when his granddaughter marries that high-tone Kyoto man, he'll be on an even higher level."

"Anyway, he retired here and can't keep himself from mischief," Toshi said.

Mas found the young man's attitude refreshing. He spoke as though he might have been a *yogore*, a dirty troublemaker, himself when he was young. "What's Children's Home?"

"Its official name is Senbazuru—you know, like the

thousand cranes for atomic-bomb survivors? It's an institution for boys who don't have parents—either by death or because they are unavailable for one reason or another. I grew up at Senbazuru. Went to Hiroshima for my education and returned to run the place. Trying to make sure that they have some kind of future."

Glancing across the road, Mas noticed a couple of the boys who had been on the ferry, paused on their bicycles. "Are those kids from your home?" he asked.

As soon as Toshi looked in their direction, they pedaled away.

"No, they're from the village on the other side of the island. Why do you ask?"

Before Mas could respond, Gohata had returned, his cell phone peeking out from his front pocket. "The police from the mainland will be coming later today." He turned his attention to Tatsuo and the other nursing-home employees, who were struggling to bring the body up onto the landing. "Leave it right there!" he called out. "And come right back up. The police will want the area to be as undisturbed as possible."

When Mas returned to the nursing home, he was surprised to see Ayako sitting at a table in the lobby. Her hair looked freshly combed and styled. Someone had meticulously groomed her, and Mas doubted Queen Ayako had done it herself.

"Good morning," she said, as if the morning was indeed good. Even though she had not been outside, Mas realized full well that she knew exactly what had transpired.

"*Ohayo*," Mas said in return. He bowed ever so slightly and felt obliged to take the other seat at the table. When his stomach growled, he realized that in spite of this morning's tragic events, he was terribly hungry.

Ayako must have heard the rumbling from his belly. "The food here is for those of us who can barely swallow. It's mush. If you want some real food, Tatsuo will have to take you back into town. No restaurants, but there's a *konbini*, at least." Mas had figured out that *konbini* was short for convenience store. In the airport, he had seen one that sold random items ranging from stationery to ham sandwiches to disposable razors.

"Orai." The sooner, the better, but Mas knew that Ayako was not going to release him yet.

"I heard that you saw the body."

Mas swallowed, his tongue clicking against his dentures. "Yah."

"What did it look like?"

Mas frowned. What a bizarre question. He must have misunderstood her.

"Itsu a boy. Teenager."

"Did it still have a face?"

Again, Mas was shocked. Haruo's big sister was going *kuru-kuru-pa*, like the rest of the crazy women in this place.

"Yah. I see him before. On the ferry."

"Really? I wonder if he was a villager? Or perhaps one

of those troublemakers in the Children's Home."

"I dunno," Mas said.

"Toshi's boys run rampant."

As Ayako kept talking and bad-mouthing all the people around her, Mas fell into a trance. He always had this inclination when someone was saying something disagreeable, but it seemed to happen more frequently in his mid-eighties. And now sleep-deprived, jet-lagged, and yes, perhaps shell-shocked, he began to actually slip out of his seat. Fortunately Tatsuo was nearby and steadied Mas in place. "Arai-*san*, maybe you should rest," he said, and Mas gratefully agreed. The walls and even the floor seemed to be moving.

Ayako seemed a bit put out. "Go then. But remember to deliver my brother's ashes to me later today."

By the time Mas reached the sliding door of his room, he thought he might collapse right then and there. Tatsuo eased him down to his futon and from there, sleep came easily. He dreamed of riding dolphins in the sea, clams and octopi at his side. His daughter, Mari, was there, too, probably only six years of age, judging from her missing front teeth. "Isn't this wonderful, Dad-dy," she called out from one of the dolphins. She was waving her arms and hands and laughing. Mas wanted to respond, but found that no sound would come out of his mouth. Something kept hitting the back of his leg, first a faint bump and then harder, so hard that the contact stung. When he looked down, it was some kind of creature—the head of a boy attached to a mini cable car.

He jerked himself awake. A dream, he told himself,

with full knowledge that the discovery of a boy's dead body was far worse. He figured that it might be around noon, Japan time. He got up and went into the bathroom across the way to take a shower. Everything in there felt institutional to him, clinical and utilitarian like a hospital. His shower was a short one.

He was now absolutely famished and had to eat as soon as possible. Closing the sliding door, he returned to the lobby and flagged down Tatsuo, who nodded.

"Arai-*san*, I was on my way to get you. I have some errands to run in town. Let's go now."

In his driver's seat on the right-hand side of the car, Tatsuo blinked repeatedly, and Mas wondered if this was a tic that he'd had all along. They rode in silence for a little while before Tatsuo finally said, "Shock. Really a shock. Nothing like this has ever happened here. I mean, we have our residents die all the time. But they are old. Not a child."

"Did you know him?"

Tatsuo was quiet for a moment. "I might have seen him before. It's hard to tell with the body being in the water. But he looked familiar."

"I saw him on the ferry," Mas announced. He didn't know why he was sharing this information so readily. Tatsuo, in his unassuming state, was easy to talk to.

"Really. You don't say. The day you arrived?"

Mas nodded.

"Maybe that's why I thought I'd seen him before." More blinking, more ferociously now. "Did he seem troubled to you?"

Mas knew what Tatsuo was asking. Did he seem like a boy who could commit suicide or hurt himself? Mas didn't want to jump to conclusions, at least not out loud. "I had no contact with him," he merely replied.

"I wonder why he was here. And why he didn't go back to where he came from by nightfall? He had to be a Hiroshima boy, I imagine."

Tatsuo continued driving south, the tops of the oyster racks now barely visible in the water. "Maybe he couldn't see properly. Fell into the water by accident."

Mas shrugged his shoulders. He appreciated Tatsuo trying to make sense of the tragedy, but in his own experience, life many times did not make sense. They finally reached the main village, and Tatsuo found a parking spot near the Shinto shrine with the patina roof. Tatsuo pointed to the *konbini* and told Mas to meet back at the car. "If I'm not here, wait in there." He gestured to an enclosed glass waiting area, which Mas assumed was air-conditioned.

While many of the homes in the area looked ramshackle and aged, aside from the satellite dishes positioned on wood balconies, the *konbini* seemed rather on the new side. It wasn't one of those chains visible from the train station, but it replicated their layout and general ambience. It had white walls with a line of shelves filled with random sundries.

As Mas approached the automatic glass doors, two cats chased a third one into his path, almost causing him to trip. They were pitiful animals, true alley cats with *kuso* coming out of their eyes and bite marks on their ears. The one being chased, a tabby that reminded Mas of his daughter's childhood pet, was in terrible shape. It was missing an eye, and, probably as a result of its compromised sight, moved in a jerky fashion. The one-eyed cat finally hid in the center of some stacked abandoned tires.

Mas entered the *konbini*, enjoying the coolness as the air conditioning enveloped his skin. He picked up a couple of sandwiches—one filled with a fried pork cutlet and the other with noodles. Genessee would not be happy with his choices, but on Ino, choices were limited. He brought his sandwiches and a couple of bottles of cold green tea to the register.

The cashier's face was ruddy with deep lines. She had a cotton scarf tied around her head, so Mas couldn't see the color of her hair. But judging from the condition of her skin, she had left her forties decades ago.

She dispensed with all niceties—no "welcome" or "*ohayo.*" In fact, she glared at Mas with suspicion as if he was inconveniencing her by frequenting her business. Well, he could certainly stare back with the same level of intensity. So he did.

The doors opened with the entrance of Tatsuo, apparently a more welcome figure. "Ah, *ohayo,*" she called out—was there even singsong in her voice? The one-eyed cat slipped in behind Tatsuo, perhaps seeking refuge from the heat or maybe the bullies.

"*Kora!*" she yelled, while grabbing hold of a broom. To make her position perfectly clear, she swiped the cat with the bristles. The cat let out a cry as it was being pushed back into the outdoor heat.

"I'll wait for you outside," Mas told Tatsuo. Carrying his bag of food, he went into the glass waiting area and began eating his breakfast. Outside he could see the placid surface of the sea. He realized he hadn't seen any signs of life in the water; no joyful flying fish or mischievous sea lions as he saw along the coast of California on the other side of the Pacific. Was life here extinguished as soon as it was dragged below? What was that boy doing here on the island?

A shriek rang out behind the waiting area; the bully cats were at it again by the Shinto shrine. The tabby cowered in a corner by some long concrete memorial tablets and the edge of a house. The black cat was on its hind legs, snarling and challenging the one-eyed feline to a duel.

Mas was not a cat lover, but Haruo definitely was. At the Flower Market where he had worked, Haruo had befriended alley cats, especially the most miserable-looking ones, plying them with treats that Spoon purchased from the market with discount coupons. After he retired, both he and Spoon fed all the stray cats in their neighborhood, much to the consternation of their neighbors. When Haruo got sick with cancer, their attention to homeless animals declined, and soon only a pitiful blind cat, black with white paws, remained on their porch.

This island tabby, its left eye missing and side marked with a horrific scar, reminded Mas of Haruo. The state of his damaged face and neck, not to mention a fake eye to replace the lost one, were remnants of the Bomb, something he could not fully hide, but he nonetheless soldiered on with the greatest optimism. Mas had once dismissed his friend as being weak, but now, more than ever, he realized that to live with hope required the highest level of courage, more courage than he himself could muster.

He finished the noodle sandwich, balling up the plastic wrapping in one fist and throwing it in the trash can. He didn't know what kind of business Tatsuo had with the cranky cashier in the *konbini*, but it was taking a long time. The cats were at it again and Mas had had enough.

The sun hitting him squarely in the face, he went straight to the right corner of the shrine. "*Yamenasai!*" he shouted for the black cat to stop, causing it to leap on a back wall and escape through a side alley. The tabby stayed frozen in place. It was straggly with matted fur and probably hadn't eaten in a few days. Against his better judgment, Mas opened up his plastic bag, pulled open the wrap for the fried pork sandwich, and tore a corner piece for the homeless cat. It was famished, judging by the way it gobbled down the bit of bread and meat. "Orai," Mas said. *That's it.* But of course that wasn't it. As he headed back to the air-conditioned waiting room, the cat followed. He closed the glass door, but the cat positioned itself right in front of the doorway, mewing furiously.

Ah, shimmata, he thought, *darn it.* Here again a little bit of kindness led to trouble. He opened the door a crack. "Go home," he admonished the cat, knowing full well that it had no home to go to.

Tatsuo was by the door of his car, his arm raised as a signal that he was ready to go.

"Yes, yes." Mas bobbed his head and, without thinking, picked the cat up by its neck and stuck it in his bag.

"I hope she wasn't too rude."

"Huh?" Mas was too concerned about the cat in the trunk to be attentive to Tatsuo.

"Kondo-*san*. The storekeeper. She doesn't like anyone who isn't from the island. Actually, she doesn't much care for anyone on the island, either. She's Gohata's wife's sister. The wife was bedridden from a mysterious illness for many years. Finally died last year."

"Gohata? Isn't that the name of the district representative?"

Tatsuo blinked several times. "You sure know a lot for arriving yesterday." His voice had an almost accusatory tone.

"He was there. On his motorbike. Where I found the boy." Mas didn't know why he had to defend himself.

"Oh, yes," Tatsuo said.

They both grew quiet again, with Mas paying nervous attention to any sounds emanating from the trunk. The cat must have known to be quiet because no mew or movement could be heard, at least from the back.

Barely able to let out a breath, he looked out his window. Part of the island was like a jungle, green with overgrown bamboo and an occasional massive camphor tree, called *kusunoki* in Japan. In any other season, the island would be pleasant.

They stopped at a T in the road where a garden had been created on the right side. There were beds of flowers and a tan shed in the back. Someone had put in the time to make this corner more tame and colorful.

"That's where we found some bones about ten years ago," Tatsuo said. "That happens sometimes. The bodies from the Bomb emerge from the land, in people's yards and construction projects. But this was a significant finding. That's why we decided to mark the spot with the garden. The tool shed has some photos of what was found."

Mas felt like spitting in distaste. Why desecrate a shed with such horrific images? It seemed like Hiroshima was all about remembering, not forgetting or moving on.

"The bones were sent to the Peace Park. That's where they belonged."

Mas pulled on the shoulder strap of his seatbelt. He felt like fleeing Japan as soon as possible. Drop off Haruo's ashes to Queen Ayako and take off. He knew that he had another five, six days in Hiroshima, but he didn't care about seeing any sights or going to the family house. Everyone he knew from before was dead. And now with the discovery of the boy in the water, more bad luck seemed to follow. Better hedge his bets and get out of Hiroshima pronto.

After Tatsuo parked the car, he popped open the trunk for Mas and excused himself, saying that he had to attend to some pressing and unexpected business. Relieved, Mas got out of the passenger seat to see what had happened to the cat in the back. Lifting up the tailgate revealed an empty food wrapper and a sated tabby, full of fried pork and bread.

"*Ara*—thatsu suppose to be my dinner," he scolded the cat, shooing it back into the plastic bag and carrying it to the side of the building.

Someone had placed two cones to block entry to the jetty. In the distance Mas could see the red of the boy's T-shirt as the body was lying there on the bamboo platform for all to see. He felt a sickness come over his stomach, intense and almost debilitating. Still clutching onto the bag, he balanced himself on the side of Tatsuo's car and made his way to a shaded walkway in back of the rest home.

There certainly were fewer table scraps on this side of the island, but then also fewer cats out for blood. He dumped the cat out from the bag and as it landed unsteadily on its feet, Mas christened it, right then and there: "Youzu Haruo." As if taking to its new name and new home, the cat ran into some bushes, perhaps chasing a tiny lizard. The *semi* had started their raspy screeches, almost serving as the backbeat of the island. Matching that monotonous rhythm, a putt-putt of a motorbike joined in.

Gohata parked a little north of the jetty and removed his helmet in the same way he had this morning. Tatsuo appeared from the nursing home and bowed his head a few times as he approached Gohata. They exchanged a few words, and Mas could have sworn that they both briefly looked his way.

They came in a small boat with red trim. Mas couldn't

tell exactly how many, but he figured out it was a sizable number based on how slowly the boat moved in the bay toward the boat landing, a little bit north of the smaller makeshift jetty.

As the boat approached, Mas saw that the officers, mostly dressed in black uniforms, were tightly packed like sardines in a can. He counted them as they emerged. *Ichi, ni, san, shi, go* . . . twelve of them in that tin can of a boat. One of them looked like a woman. The last ones to disembark carried the most equipment. Gohata met them on the landing, bowing at least three times to the police officers in the front. He was prepared with his business card, which he offered to them with both hands.

The officers first set up a white tent on the soft ground by the water.

Mas watched this from a bench in the shade of a camphor tree. He thought perhaps he was invisible, but he was wrong, because after some time, Tatsuo came over to deliver a message: "Arai-*san*, the police want to talk with you."

The police had set up their operations in the back room of the nursing-home office. On this side of the island, where else could they go? Exposing the investigation to the children at the Senbazuru Children's Home was unacceptable, especially since they might be the ones with the most pertinent information, explained Tatsuo. His face was flushed and his blinking took on a strange musical rhythm. *Pachi, pachi, pachi,* pause, *pachi, pachi, pachi,* pause.

Mas entered the back office. The papers that had once been stacked on the conference room table had been removed. Three detectives sat on different sides of the table, all facing Mas, who took the only other available seat.

A video camera had been set up on the other side of Mas. Another officer, wearing headphones, stood behind the camera.

The one who sat immediately across from Mas seemed the most senior. He had salt-and-pepper hair that stuck out like the spines of a hedgehog. He carefully turned each page in Mas's passport. "You are American?"

Mas nodded.

"Why are you here in Ino?"

"Came to see my friend's sister. Ayako Mukai. She's staying here." On Mas's left, a detective with a baby face feverishly scribbled on his pad. Undoubtedly Ayako would be getting an official visit before the day was over.

"I think saw that boy before. On the boat."

"What makes you say that?" The detectives focused intently on Mas's face. The cameraman adjusted some settings on his equipment.

" 'San Francisco.' Was that on his T-shirt?"

The detectives looked at each other again. "What can you tell us about him?"

"I don't know much. I am an outsider." And he was, for once, so happy to be one.

"Was he with someone?"

"He sat by himself," Mas said. He said he wasn't sure if he was part of the gang of boys running around the Ujina landing and being disruptive. Mas normally tried to ignore groups of *urusai* boys instead of paying attention to what obnoxious things they were doing or saying. "I was with a girl."

The detectives exchanged glances. *Bakayaro*, Mas wanted to yell at them. *It's not what you are thinking.* "Mukai-*san* knows. Her student's daughter picked me up from the station. Her name, Thea." He couldn't remember her last name.

"Maybe she knows the boy," the baby-faced detective interjected.

Mas doubted it but said nothing.

"Who else was on the ferry?" the senior detective asked.

"These other boys. About his age. They ran into the village after we landed."

"Children," the third detective, who had remained silent until now, said almost disparagingly, as if he'd had bad experiences dealing with youth.

They asked a few more questions, purely perfunctory and nothing earth-shattering. At first Mas's heart was pumping hard, but now he was completely calm, almost bored. It was obvious that he wasn't a suspect.

When Mas finally emerged from the makeshift interrogation room, Thea was sitting at the table in the lobby. He was surprised to see her, as she had mentioned something about going to work today.

"I heard what happened," she said. "How terrible." She was drinking a canned iced coffee, most likely purchased from the vending machine inside the cafeteria.

"When youzu come?"

"Oh, I came on the ferry from the other side. I was able

to get a ride in from Tatsuo-*san*."

Mas frowned. After driving him into the village, Tatsuo said he had to attend to business. Why was Thea lying?

"By the way, Mukai-*san* is asking about her brother's ashes."

"Yah, bring it right away." He got up from his seat. Once this task was complete, he would be on his way, whether or not the police officers approved.

Mas couldn't help but smile a little as he walked down the wide corridor. He imagined being back in the embrace of Genessee, her musty scent so pure and earthy. Mari would come by, excerpts of her latest documentary viewable on her laptop. Mari's husband, the Dodgers groundskeeper, would brief him on the latest gossip about the baseball team, and Takeo, his grandson, would show him photos from the latest judo match he'd won. Life was utterly mundane and simple—one day much like the day before, but Mas relished its consistency because there'd been times in his life when he could not depend on it.

He slid open the door to his room. His futon was still out, unfolded like he left it. But when he went to retrieve Haruo's ashes from in front of the yellow silk rose, he discovered that the bag was gone.

Chapter Three

How could Haruo's ashes be missing?

Mas looked underneath the table and behind the television screen. He pulled the sheets off the futon and examined the top comforter and futon mattress. Nothing. Had he returned it back to his suitcase for some reason? Whenever he was sleep-deprived, he did strange, illogical things, like put his keys in the refrigerator. He shook everything out of his suitcase and searched every compartment and zippered bag. No bag of ashes anywhere.

Then Mas began to search the entire room. He had no idea why it would suddenly be in a far corner or in the closet where the bedding was stored, but he left no space unexamined. Even his dirty socks and underwear merited a second look.

With the sheets bunched up and his clothing strewn on the bare futon and tatami floor, Mas felt completely dejected. He sunk to his knees. How could this have happened? He had one task and one task only, to deliver half of his friend's ashes to the sister in Hiroshima, and he had failed terribly.

There was a knocking on the wooden sliding door. "Arai-*san*, are you okay?" The girl's high-pitched voice was like torture to Mas.

He managed to make it to the door and opened it a crack. "I'zu not feelin' so good," Mas told Thea. "Tell Mukai-*san* I see her tomorrow."

"Can I help in any way? I can send for a doctor."

"No, sleepy."

"Of course, of course. I completely understand. You've had a shocking experience after such a tiring day of travel. Rest, *Ojisan*, please rest."

Mas bowed, relieved when Thea left. Closing the sliding door firmly shut, he took a deep breath. What the hell was he going to do? He couldn't think straight with his room ransacked like this. He carefully folded his clean clothes back in his suitcase and even folded up his futon into thirds and pushed it into the bedding closet.

And then he remembered. The strange woman in his room that first night. If she wasn't a housekeeper, she must have been the one who took Haruo's ashes. But who was she? Mas had no name, not even a good way to identify her. An old Japanese woman. Like eighty percent of people living in the home.

Surely Tatsuo could help him. But he didn't want to encounter the detectives again, so he thought that he would have to wait for at least a few hours. Even if they had chartered their own boat, there was no place to stay on the island. The police officers had to go home eventually.

At around six, Mas slid open his door. It had been an
hour since he'd heard the workers wheel carts down the linoleum floors. He listened intently with his better ear, the
left one. Just a Japanese announcer on a television broad-
cast. It seemed safe to get to the office.

Thankfully, Tatsuo was by himself behind the counter,
applying a *hanko*, seal, on a piece of paper.

"They left," Mas observed, more than asked. The police
seemed to have cleared the premises.

"Yes. A couple of hours ago. They took the body with
them."

Mas exhaled. The investigation was all over.

"Can I help you with something, Arai-*san*?"

"Do you have a house cleaner?"

"We do have a janitor."

"Would he have cleaned my room sometime today?"

Tatsuo shook his head. "The guest rooms are off limits.
What has happened? Are you missing something?"

Mas hesitated. He wasn't a hundred percent sure if he
could trust Tatsuo. What if he took this information and
went straight to Ayako? It would be the ultimate shame,
haji. Here he had traveled six thousand miles, and to return
to Los Angeles without completing his duty? And Spoon
had paid for his travel and then some? How could he look
into the eyes of Haruo's widow ever again?

But without Tatsuo's help, Mas definitely would be
lost. "An old lady took something of mine," he finally said.
"She was in my room in the middle of the night. The night
I arrived."

"What was her appearance? And what did she take?"

Mas struggled to describe the woman. "It almost seemed she had no eyes. She was wearing a *chanchanko*. And she said something about people lying to her." He didn't mention what was stolen.

Tatsuo nodded. "Sounds like Kondo-*Obasan*. She's the *konbini* owner's mother; she does things like this. But the only thing is—she was moved out of the home this morning."

Mas thought that his heart had stopped, right then and there. "Why? Did something happen to her?"

Tatsuo cleaned the end of his *hanko*, the orange ink seeping into a white tissue. He seemed more intent on his task than answering Mas's question. "Ah, well, I can't get into details."

Mas wanted to shake Tatsuo. Who cared about privacy at a time like this?

Tatsuo must have sensed Mas's agitation. "Let's check her room," he said. "What are we looking for?"

Mas rubbed the back of his head. It felt painful to confess it audibly. "The ashes. Mukai-*san*'s brother's ashes. They were in a small bag."

"*Soka*," Tatsuo said, *I understand*. He nodded in the direction of the hallway and walked swiftly out.

The woman had lived on the other side of the facility, and judging from the low beds and increasing number of residents in wheelchairs, Mas figured out that these patients were less ambulatory.

More of the rooms seemed to hold at least two beds,

but Kondo-*Obasan*'s was a single. It, too, had a view of the ocean. Kondo-*Obasan*, like Ayako, was undoubtedly a big shot, or at least a big shot's relative.

The room was empty; only the dirty, disheveled sheets were a sign that someone had stayed there. Tatsuo pulled the sheets from the mattress, but nothing emerged. Mas stuck his hands in between the mattress and bed frame, and again found nothing.

Tatsuo balled up the sheets and then, after checking for anything left behind or hidden, chucked them into the hamper. Mas examined every corner of the room, even running his hand inside a tissue box. "There's nothing here," Tatsuo said, announcing the obvious. "Gohata-*san* packed everything up and moved her out in a few hours. It was quite sudden." He absorbed Mas's reaction. "Yes, the same Gohata-*san*. That's Kondo-*Obasan*'s son-in-law."

The district representative seemed to be everywhere, his presence like a spider's, spinning a web of secrets wherever he traveled.

"It's not unusual for the family to do this. Kondo-*Obasan* was just brought in overnight last May. No advance warning."

"Can you tell me where her new nursing home is?"

Tatsuo hesitated. "I'm not sure if I should get involved."

Short of getting down on his hands and knees, Mas implored, "I will not say anything. You know my shame."

Tatsuo nodded, making Mas feel even worse, because he was confirming the depth of his *haji*. "I guess I could call for you and check."

They returned to the office, where Tatsuo got on the phone. It sounded like he was calling *konbini* Kondo, and making up an excuse that he needed to send some additional paperwork to the facility where she was staying.

After hanging up, he went on the computer to find the institution's exact address. He wrote all the information in *kanji* as well as in hiragana, one of the two Japanese phonetic alphabets, treating Mas almost like an elementary school child. He might as well have, because Mas's written Japanese was about at that level.

"Sank you, *ne*," Mas said in English, and then repeating it in Japanese. "I am truly indebted to you."

"The first boat will arrive on this side of the island at eight in the morning," Tatsuo said, explaining that a smaller vessel, the one that had earlier transported the police officers, only made three trips a day, while the larger ferry had a more full schedule. Tatsuo would be leaving on the last boat tonight and wouldn't be back for two days. Tuesday was the island's annual commemoration of the atomic bombing, two days before the massive one at the Peace Park in Hiroshima on August 6. He offered Mas something in a green bag with handles. "My lunch. You must be hungry. I've had no appetite today. You probably need this more than I do."

With knowledge that the boy's dead body was now off the island, Mas felt like he could breathe. He went outside through a side door, Tatsuo's bag in tow. "Haruo," he called out. And then a little louder, "Haruo." The sun was going down quickly, yet the heat was still present, not blazing but enough to feel unpleasant.

Mas sat down on a bench and while swatting mosquitos away from his ankles, devoured Tatsuo's slightly stale lunch. There were some tough bits of boneless fried chicken, *karaage*, and misshapen rice balls. Mas wondered where Haruo the cat was. Had he seized a lost hermit crab by the shore? Finally *nyaa nyaa*, Haruo came around through some side bushes, stalking his new territory like a proud miniature tiger. Mas was relieved that the one-eyed cat seemed so happy in his new surroundings. Luckily, there was some leftover chicken, which Mas showered upon the hard-packed ground. Haruo wasted no time in making the morsels disappear.

That night sleep came easily and Mas didn't wake until past eight o'clock in the morning Hiroshima time. *Chikusho*, he cursed, but he knew that another ferry was due in an hour. Quickly brushing the few real teeth he had and inserting his dentures, he was ready to go.

The landing was completely uncovered, so he opted to take a seat on a bench underneath a metal awning. He thought he was alone, but then came the voice of a woman: "So many dead people here."

She walked over from the jetty, holding an open umbrella, its shade darkening her face. She looked thirty, which meant she was probably at least five years older, with a bob of honey-blond hair, most likely dyed, and a chin that came to a point. Her small, hooded eyes looked strange, even a bit reptilian. Mas almost feared that there might be other bodies floating in the tide.

The woman closed her umbrella and sat down on the bench next to Mas, who wished he could get up and blend into the environment. But a deserted island provided a man with few options to blend.

"So hot," she said, fanning herself with her right hand and attempting to preserve her thick layer of makeup. "I don't know how a person can stand living here."

"Just visiting." Not that it was the stranger's business, but Mas surrendered that much personal information.

"It's horrible, isn't it?" she said. "That's why I didn't want Sora to come. Forbade his father to bring him. But he never listens to me."

Sora, sky. *What an odd name*, Mas thought. *Is this what is popular these days in Japan?*

"Sora was my son. He was the one who was discovered here."

Of course, Mas immediately understood what she was saying. He could not find the words to respond.

"They told me last night. I had to come here, on the first ferry out of Ujina. I had to see where it happened."

"I found him," Mas finally said.

"What?"

"I found him in the water."

Her eyes welled up. She blinked, releasing tears, stripes down her powdered cheeks.

"Was he alive then?"

Mas shook his head. He probably hadn't been for

some time.

The young mother took out a fabric tissue holder from her bag, but it was completely empty, probably from a morning of crying. She pressed the sides of her eyes, as if that would stop her tears. "I never liked coming here. I told Hideki that. Hideki, that's Sora's father. I told him not to bring Sora here. Sora barely left his room, and now to take him on a boat to an island. But he never listened to me. I could never stop Hideki from doing anything," she said. She said it in a way that made Mas think that she wasn't talking only about this incident.

"We were on the same boat coming here," he told her.

Surprisingly, the mother didn't react much to this news. "Was he with someone?" she asked casually, as if she might know who he was with.

"He sat alone." Mas was still unsure about Sora's connection to the other boys.

The young mother took a deep breath and declared, "My son didn't do this to himself. I know that's what the police are saying. That I'm an unfit single mother, that I wasn't keeping track of my son. But his father was supposed to check on him while I was at work." She explained that Sora had texted her that he was playing an online game with one of his friends. The police had found his cell phone in his pocket, and all the data was lost from being submerged in the water. But investigators were working to retrieve text messages from the phone company.

Mas stared at his watch, wishing that he knew how to change the time.

The woman's jaw tightened for a moment before she started speaking again. "Someone forced him to do it, I'm sure of it. He was not the type to go off and do things on his own. He was afraid of heights, and even water."

But then why did he travel to the island in the first place? And why did he debark on the other side of the island? He would have needed some kind of transportation to get over to the east side in this heat. Something didn't add up.

Based on his mathematic calculations, it was close to nine now, and he rose to check the water. Sure enough, the small boat with the red trim was zipping through the ocean toward the landing.

"Here, let me give you my phone number if something comes to you about that ferry ride."

"Don't have a phone," Mas said, relieved that he didn't have one.

The woman went through her bag and brought out a business card. "Well, then. This is where we live on Nagarekawa-*dori*, at least for now," she said, forgetting that it was just her now.

Mas had remembered that lively street from his childhood. Bike riders, horses pulling carts and men pushing carts, row after row of storefronts, and round lights hung above the street. It was magical, quite a difference from the *inaka*, the countryside, where rice paddies were surrounded by high hills.

Mas accepted the card, an advertisement for a ramen eatery.

"It's the apartment above the ramen shop in room 403. My name is Tani. Tani Rei." She then asked, "And your name?"

"Arai." Although she had offered her first name, Rei, Mas felt no need to reciprocate with his. The given name was just incidental anyway. In Japan, there were longtime friends who were uncertain of each other's first names.

"The police want to close the case quickly. Say that it was the case of a poor boy unsupervised by his divorced mother. But it cannot be closed so simply," Rei said. "Nothing is that simple."

The boat was now docked at the landing. "My ferry," he said.

"Yes, make your escape," Rei said. "I plan on returning on the noon boat. After I collect some flowers and throw them into the water. While his body is no longer here, his soul might be. Do you not agree?"

Mas did not answer. Not bothering to say goodbye, he trudged down to the landing, where a couple of other people had assembled. He gave the skipper a few of his coins. On this less-populated side of the island, the vessel was much more humble and small, definitely a one-man operation.

He sat inside opposite the two other passengers, but he felt a bit claustrophobic. As the skipper, a middle-aged man with a potbelly, powered up the boat, Mas chose instead to sit on the small outside deck. The salt water misted his face, but it was refreshing, as if Hiroshima was entering his pores. He hoped to see some kind of life in the sea—porpoises, flying fish, anything—but apparently they weren't the type of creatures who lived close to the surface.

He wondered about what Rei said. Was she just a grief-stricken mother spouting out madness to alleviate her guilt? Or was there something to her suspicions?

He pictured her picking flowers, perhaps from that garden down by the school that commemorated the discovery of the buried bodies. She spoke about her son's soul. Mas was raised to be a believer in Mother Nature, to believe that trees, plants, and rocks could indeed have a soul like people do. But after he married the churchgoing Genessee, Jesus had come into his life. As he understood it—and there was a lot that he didn't understand—Jesus was a samurai who accepted death not on his master's behalf, but on that of those lower, the peasants and the prostitutes. It was a strange religion, but one that secretly delighted him. At one of the services at Genessee's church, the pastor called God a gardener, and Mas thought he had misheard him. But later Genessee opened up her Holy Book and showed Mas that it was true. God the Father was indeed a gardener.

Mas really didn't understand prayer, but from the deck of that speeding boat, he released one for the boy. Even if it didn't reach God, he thought, maybe there was a place where prayers gathered and rested, waiting for the best time to make their appearance.

Once they reached Ujina, the boat stopped at a pier east of the large ferry building. Luckily, a black taxi was parked at the curb and a driver ran and opened the door for Mas. He gave the driver the paper on which Tatsuo had written the address of the nursing-home, and they were on their way in a few minutes.

Mas wondered what he would say to Kondo-*Obasan*, if she would even recognize him. He didn't know how he would be able to search her belongings, but he had to at least try. He had no choice.

The assisted-care facility, a nondescript three-story building, was in the neighborhood of a few museums and the high school that his first wife, Chizuko, had attended. Across the street was Shukkei-en, a public garden that Mas faintly remembered. It was odd to think that Shukkei-en, with its Bomb-torn tree limbs and scorched plants, could have somehow been brought back to life, but based on the sign outside a gate, it was open for business.

Mas paid the fare and got out of the taxi, wondering how in the world he would pull this off.

Opening the glass door, he entered the reception area, which was staffed by a woman in her twenties. "Excuse me, but I am here to see Kondo-*Obasan*," he said in the most proper Japanese that he could manage.

"Are you family?"

He shook his head no.

The receptionist puckered her lips as if she had bit into a lemon. She bowed slightly. "One moment please," she said before getting on the phone.

Mas couldn't hear exactly what she was saying. Only that his request was causing a bit of a problem.

The elevator dinged and opened to reveal one of the few people that Mas had gotten to know on this short trip: the girl, Thea, wearing a white polo shirt and a white mask that she had pulled down underneath her chin.

"Arai-*san*, what are you doing here?"

"What youzu doin' here?"

"I work here."

Mas didn't have time to process this coincidence. He had only one purpose right now. "Izu come to talk to dat lady, Aunt Kondo," he announced.

"May I ask why? We have strict instructions that no one aside from family is supposed to visit her." She pulled Mas closer to the door and farther away from the receptionist.

"She saysu sumptin to me," he said. "Sumptin that don't sound right."

"I wouldn't pay her any mind. She has Alzheimer's. She usually doesn't even remember her own relatives."

"Lemme talk to her for few minutes. I'zu no cause no problems," he said, knowing that he really couldn't guarantee that.

"I'm due a break in a few minutes, Arai-*san*. Just wait here and I'll come down."

Mas nodded. Because of the heat, he stayed in the small waiting area, with the receptionist giving him sour expressions about every ten minutes.

Finally the elevator dinged again and Thea reemerged without the mask fastened around her ears. She gestured that they should go outside, and they sat on a side table in the shade.

"What is this all about? Why do you need to speak to Kondo-*Obasan* so badly?"

Mas came close to confessing that he had lost Haruo's ashes. The words had moved from his belly to his throat and to his tongue. But he couldn't do it. Thea was a female and so young. She could be his granddaughter. How could he admit his failings to a person like this? Besides, there was no doubt she would go straight to Ayako with this news of his failure.

He bit down on his dentures, offering no information.

"This doesn't have to do with that boy, does it? The one who killed himself? You couldn't have done anything to prevent it, you know. The police say he's from a very unstable family. A couple of detectives came and spoke to me this morning. I didn't even notice him on the boat, but I heard that you remembered him from our ride." She adjusted her ponytail. "His parents are divorced and the mother sounds horrible."

Mas couldn't help but frown. Did the police divulge all this to Thea?

"The father had apparently been on the island during Golden Week in May. Doing some work on a villager's house. Brought the boy with him."

Thea seemed to know a lot about the gossip on the island—especially for an outsider. Maybe she was one of these people who had to constantly dribble out any information that was presented to her. Mas decided to test her knowledge about Ayako and her quest to be reunited with Haruo. "Whyzu Ayako-*san* wants her brotha's ashes so much? Kinda don't make sense."

She shrugged. "Mukai-*san* is tough to figure out. I know Haruo was the last of her brothers and sisters to die. She always talks about being the only one around."

"No way to talk to Kondo-*Obasan*? Take a quick look around?"

"I'm sorry, Arai-*san*. I don't think the family will allow it."

A buzz sounded from her shirt pocket. She took the call, responding, "*Hai, hai, hai.* I must go." She rose from the table. "I'll get you a taxi to take you back to Ujina."

"Orai, orai. It's fine. I'd like to stay here for longer."

"Really? Well, if you need my help, you know where I'll be."

Mas nodded.

As she disappeared into the box of the assisted-care facility, he remained seated, trying to figure out his next move.

So the case of Sora Tani was solved, just like that. The boy had killed himself. What a tragic end to such a young life. This wasn't the first time that Mas had encountered the dead body of a teenager. There had been so many here in Hiroshima that August of 1945. His classmates, forced to work at the Hiroshima train station. During those last years of the war, there was no school. Men were disappearing and boys too young to be drafted still had to help the war effort by doing manual labor. Names that he hadn't spoken in years came to his lips: Kenji, Riki, Joji.

He murmured more prayers before stopping himself. What was he doing? He was really going *kuru-kuru-pa* now. He took a deep breath. He would have to confess to the young student nurse. Get her help in searching for Haruo's ashes. He came here as a good-for-nothing gaijin, a foreigner, an outsider, anyway. He might as well fulfill all the low expectations that everyone had of him.

He returned to the waiting room and once again stood before the sour-looking receptionist, who instructed him to wait. After five minutes, he couldn't stand it any longer. Without telling her where he'd be, he crossed the street to Shukkei-en. As always, when he needed to think clearly, he gravitated toward green.

After paying the admission fee, Mas entered the grounds. His heart was pounding because he remembered running through here when he was maybe six or seven. The tall, fat *toro* lanterns that today reminded him of stone snowmen. The expansive flat pond and the two bridges that joined the islands together. One bridge was a brilliant vermilion red with grand black knobs that he and his brothers used to grab hold of. The pond below was stocked with white, orange, and black koi that opened and closed their mouths, begging for food. Farmhouses with thatched straw roofs, stone mushroom chairs . . . all of that was there in the faithful restoration. Luckily, he had Mari's camera in his jeans pocket, so he snapped a few photos for old time's sake.

When he reached the side of the garden next to Kyobashi River, he stumbled across a large rock engraved with some kind of Japanese writing. It was shaded in darkness and had none of the vibrancy of the rest of the garden. He saw three rectangular stones leading up to it, and two metal vases holding red peonies on the sides as offerings. Reading the old kanji as *irei*, or comforting the souls of the dead, Mas wasn't surprised to see a sign explaining that a dead body had been found buried from the blast at this spot during the renovation, followed by the discovery of sixty-four more in the 1980s.

At this point, Mas was ready to leave. The hedges, *toro* lanterns, and energetic koi had sustained him and distracted him from his problems, but this memorial reminded him that it was still Hiroshima. New plants, their roots shallow, could not reverse the damage of radiation and black rain. Architects and workers had restored the garden to what it looked like seventy, a hundred, or even more years ago, but it was like a superficial mask covering the darkness that was below.

He made his way over wooden bridges and cobblestone surfaces before he reached the gift store and connected snack shop. A table fan circulated, and he brushed away the sweat above his lip. Seeing a handwritten sign advertising shaved ice, he decided to take a brief break to cool down his body.

At one of the small square tables, Mas ate his green tea snow cone while looking through the images of the photos he had taken. After putting on his reading glasses, he pressed the back arrow button once, twice, and so on until he reached the photos he had taken on the ferry going over to Ino. He had not been paying much attention where he was aiming the lens, and now he saw that he'd accidentally captured some of the other passengers, specifically Sora in his red T-shirt. The image on the screen on the back of the camera was small, smaller than his palm, but holding it at the right distance, he saw that Sora was not alone. He was seated next to one of the boys from the village. The other boy was larger and heavier, wearing a tan shirt. Mas could have sworn that he recognized the same boy among the young bicyclists observing the retrieval of Sora's body the next morning.

Sora had not been alone then. And this boy knew him well enough to be seated next to him. Curious. Did the police have this information?

From his pocket Mas took out the business card for the ramen shop, located in the lively area of Nagarekawa-*dori*. Maybe if he showed the picture to the mother, she would recognize the boy Sora had been talking to. And maybe, like she said, Sora didn't die the way the police said he did.

Chapter Four

B y the time he walked out of Shukkei-en, the sky had turned dark, and warm raindrops wet his head and lashes. It was actually a relief from the unbearable heat, so instead of hailing a cab, Mas opted to walk. He was starting to get his bearings, and even though everything in the new Hiroshima was updated and fancy, he noticed signs with old photographs from the 1940s displayed here and there. They served to jog his memory, breadcrumbs on a trail of the past.

A green streetcar was waiting at a stop, and without even asking where it was going, Mas got on. The Hiroden system had been around since the 1940s, and Mas thought he even saw some cars from that era still in operation. This particular one was heading south, and that was where he wanted to be.

Hiroshima had been designed like a grid—his father had once explained that it was that way to accommodate the needs of the daimyo, the feudal lord. In those samurai days, there was a district that made fresh tofu, and a few others that sold fish. Once there was even a section that handled the sale of firearms; the young Mas found that especially interesting.

In that way, Hiroshima reminded him of downtown Los Angeles: the Flower Market next to the Produce Market next to Toy Town and then Little Tokyo and City Hall. Everything was contained, for the most part, in these municipal blocks. It was pretty easy to know when you'd gone too far.

The streetcar made a stop at Hatchobori and he noticed passengers, mostly middle-aged women, get up. Hatchobori, Mas remembered that street. And Fukuya, the grand multilevel department store, had been in this area. He and his classmates had once been chased out of that building for pulling the clothes off of a mannequin. After the Bomb, the outside concrete structure miraculously stayed intact, but its beautiful interior with all of the expensive furnishings and merchandise, was scorched away, leaving an empty black hole. In that emptiness, sick people were brought. Only instead of getting better, they got worse. One of Mas's friends—the ringleader of the mannequin mischief, in fact—was quarantined there and his brother told Mas of the nightmare of blood that came out of the sick when they went to the bathroom. Dysentery, the health experts thought. But they didn't know anything about the effects of the Bomb and radiation then.

Following the other passengers' lead, Mas got off the streetcar. From the platform in the middle of the street, he looked up to see a white multilevel building as grand as the

Fukuya before World War II. The rain had now mostly subsided, and the pedestrians were collapsing their umbrellas and shaking water from the backs of their jacket collars.

In this moment of nostalgic reverie, Mas felt bold. He asked a woman carrying a large bag stamped Fukuya, "Where is Nagarekawa-*dori*?"

"Just around the corner," she said.

Instead of going straight on the long boulevard of Nagarekawa-*dori*, Mas wandered. His body, his adolescent core, knew this grid, and he didn't need to think too much about where he was. And another thing, he was hungry. He refused to swallow another bite of a *konbini* sandwich, especially with the tasty smells wafting through the street. Further teasing him was the plastic food on display: a replicated bowl of steaming noodles with slices of pink-swirl fishcakes, and *oyakodonburi*, chicken and egg over a bowl of rice.

Before he knew it, he was in front of Okonomiyaki-mura, an actual village of his favorite Hiroshima soul food, the savory pancake: a layer of pan-fried pork slices over noodles, held together with a crepe-like dough and topped with green onion and seaweed, smothered with mayonnaise and a special *okonomiyaki* sauce. Mas had to moisten his lips so that the saliva didn't drip down his chin. He went up the stairs and was met with stand after stand offering slight variations, including additions of mochi, cheese, and oysters (presumably the kind that would not kill him). He sat in the first available seat in front of a flat grill. People from Hiroshima said that the dirtier the *okonomiyaki* establishment, the better, and based on the bits of food still remaining in the corners of the grill, this one would be a candidate for the best. As it turned out, the food was good enough, and good enough was perfect for Mas.

Grabbing a toothpick on his way out, he felt reenergized, ready to hang out, be *bura-bura*, aimless, on the streets of Hiroshima. When his feet met the pavement, he knew exactly where he was going.

When he finally entered Nagarekawa-*dori*, he couldn't quite figure out whether he was in the center of a red-light district. There were plenty of bars, pachinko halls, and men in cheap, shiny suits passing out postcards featuring head shots of young women. Yet in between those establishments were flower shops, pasta houses, and shoe repair services. Unemployed *yogore* strutted down the street next to elegant older women in high heels carrying expensive shopping bags. It was such a strange confluence of people and businesses. What a place to raise a child.

Referring to Rei's business card, Mas was finally able to find the ramen shop at the end of the street as it intersected with Heiwa-*dori*. The eatery was nothing special, a greasy spoon for bachelors. He didn't go in, but stood a few feet from the doorway, observing what he could through the long, rectangular slats of the hanging cloth called *noren*. He saw a simple metal counter lined with bar chairs. Definitely a place that drunkards frequented either before or after a night of raucous drinking.

The ramen shop was on the bottom of a dilapidated building. Tiles were literally falling off its sides, exposing gigantic cracks in the concrete. An open glass door revealed rows of mailboxes. Surely this would be the entrance to the Tani apartment.

An elevator that could barely hold more than two people took Mas to the fourth floor. He saw a bicycle in the hallway next to 403. Was it the boy's? This being Japan, the bike was not locked or secured to anything.

He knocked on the door, a clang of metal. If Rei was home, she would have heard. Mas checked his watch and calculated the difference in time. It was almost six o'clock. Perhaps she had gone out to dinner or shopping.

"Are you with the moving company?" A man about sixty years of age stood behind him. His oily hair was jet black, but Mas figured that it was dyed. He wore a thick gold bracelet around his wrist, and his face was beet red. He reeked of sake, too.

Mas shook his head. "I'm looking for Tani-*san*."

"Everybody is looking for her. I heard police was here yesterday. She's a piece of work."

It was obvious that this man, probably the apartment manager, had no idea what had happened to Sora.

Just then a door to one of the apartments opened. It was a young woman with a swollen belly. "Ah, Uchida-*san*, there you are. Our air-con isn't working properly, and with the baby on the way, this is a big problem."

"Yes, yes, I know, I know. I just got back in town this morning. I'm dealing with Tani-*san*'s situation right now. She was supposed to move out by the first of the month. This is a real pain."

The man turned his attention back to Mas. "Are you

related to her in some way?"

"No."

"Not a boyfriend, right?"

Mas scowled. "Of course not. I'm just an acquaintance."

"Good. I'd think she'd sunk to a new low."

"Well, none of that has anything to do with me," the pregnant woman interjected. "All I know is this needs to be fixed as soon as possible. I wouldn't want to call the owner." With that, she slammed the door.

The manager mouthed something silently at the door, and based on his ugly expression, it was nothing good. "See what I have to put up with? Tani-*san* is really quite a burden. I told her she had to pay me the 200,000 yen she owes or get out. Her son never leaves the apartment. I shudder to think what it looks like in there. I can't even get in because she added a deadbolt. Without my permission." He looked like he was going to fall down, but he balanced himself with one hand on the hallway wall. "You've never been inside, have you?"

Mas shook his head.

"That doesn't surprise me. All of her gentlemen callers have to stay outside. Even the kid's only friend, this weirdo kid with the bug eyes—I think his father owns that manga and video game store on Hondori—doesn't even get in. They have to talk through the door."

He stumbled toward the back of hallway. "I come home to this, can you believe it," he murmured to himself. "My work is never done."

Disgusted, Mas opted for the stairs instead of the

elevator. With this kind of manager, it was a safer bet. Once on the first floor, he tried to figure out where to go next. Through the glass panel, he saw a set of vending machines across the street. He was thirsty. While on his way to get something cold to drink, he was surprised to see Toshi Ikeda of Senbazuru emerging from the ramen shop. He was accompanied by a taller and thinner man about his same age. This companion had a long, expressionless face that almost looked like a mask. Even when he was talking, his lips barely parted, and the top of his face remained motionless.

Mas wondered what Toshi was doing here, at the exact spot where the boy, Sora Tani, lived. Toshi hadn't mentioned that he'd known the victim, at least not when the body was first discovered.

As they stood outside the ramen shop, the tall man took out a cigarette from his shirt pocket. As he held it in his lips, he was saying something to Toshi. Toshi nodded and the man offered him a crushed pack from the same pocket.

Their cigarettes lit, they sauntered up Nagarekawa-*dori*, underneath neon lights that were just flickering on. Mas, curious, followed. They finally walked downstairs into one of the bars.

Outside was a sandwich board displaying head shots of eight women, all adorned with brightly colored flowers in their hair. They all looked middle-aged and more Filipino than Japanese. He had attended one or two hostess bars in Los Angeles—all visits tied to his amateur investigations—and he didn't relish descending into that world today. Again, *shikataganai*. If he wanted to know what these two men were up to, what alternative did he have? As soon as he went down the stairs into the bar, he regretted it. It was a dark, sad space, with red and green bulbs placed in light fixtures, a weak attempt to add an air of festivity. Instead it seemed like Christmas in hell.

He wasn't sure where the two men had disappeared to. There were only a couple of others at the bar and he joined them, ordering a beer from a middle-aged hostess wearing not only a silk flower in her hair but a necklace of mini conch shells.

Immediately after his beer arrived, he felt someone's presence behind him. "Arai-*san*, I didn't know you were a drinking man."

Toshi didn't seem surprised to see Mas in this hostess bar in the Nagarekawa district. He was indeed the master of the poker face. There was no coincidence here, and they both knew it.

"Come, please join us." Toshi motioned to a dark corner away from the lights. They sat at a round glass table on bulgy seats with no backs. The thin man smashed his cigarette into an ashtray and promptly took out a new cigarette.

"Hideki-*kun*, this is Arai from America. He was the one who found Sora."

Toshi's straightforward introduction would sound innocuous to anyone who didn't know. Hideki was the name the mother had mentioned back at the pier in Ino. This must be Sora's father.

Hideki, on the other hand, was going through his own realization. He closed his eyes tighter and tighter until tears squeezed out onto his cheeks. He left the still-smoldering cigarette on the edge of the ashtray and slid off his seat. Standing in front of Mas, he bowed stiffly, his hands at his side. "I'm so sorry to cause you such inconvenience. I am indebted to you."

He kept his head lowered, and Mas couldn't take it anymore. What did he do after all? He saw something bright red bobbing in the ocean and called for help. Sora had been dead for some time, at least hours.

"It wasn't anything," Mas finally said, hoping this would cause the man to stand upright. "Anyone would have done the same."

Now in addition to tears, clear snot was running down Hideki's face. He was a mess, and Mas couldn't blame him. Toshi handed him a gauze handkerchief and Hideki bobbed his head again. After he wiped his face, Mas realized that what he'd thought to be a face without emotion was actually one swollen with grief.

"I shouldn't have gone to that party. I should have stayed with him," Hideki said to his friend. "If I was with him—"

"Stop. No more. You can't be blaming yourself. Where was she that night? If she was home, she'd know that he'd gone missing."

Hideki asked to borrow Toshi's phone. He had mislaid his somewhere.

Toshi sighed and handed a cell phone to him. "Don't lose that. I told you not to spend so much money on such an expensive one."

"Excuse me," Hideki said, making his way outside, where there was presumably better reception.

As soon as Sora's father was out of earshot, Toshi's demeanor completely flip-flopped. "What the hell are you trying to prove, old man?" he said, his mouth twisted in a sneer. "I know you didn't appear out of nowhere. Have you been following me? Who sent you here?"

To watch Toshi's transformation in a matter of seconds stunned Mas, and he found it difficult to recover. "The mother," he finally said. "Rei. She told me that she and the boy lived in this neighborhood. But I thought she was divorced."

"How do you know Rei?"

"She was at the island this morning. She was suffering, too."

"Don't let her fool you. She is the master of manipulation. A master actor."

You are pretty good yourself, Mas thought.

"She's happy Sora is dead. He was a burden to her. He's *hikikomori*, you know?"

Mas furrowed his brow.

"*Hikikomori*, it's all over Japan. Even with some of my boys at Senbazuru. They are shut-ins. Can't deal with the outside world. Can only relate through the internet and video games."

Rei had not used this term, but she and the manager had said something about him rarely leaving his room. Mas hadn't realized that this was some kind of medical condition.

"She held him close to her because she could hurt

Hideki that way. He worshipped his son; even made sure that he lived nearby after the divorce. Look at him now. I was worried that Hideki might kill himself, too. He's such a mess that he's lost his phone, so I had to come all the way over here to make sure he's okay."

"The mother doesn't think he did it."

"Is that what she said?" Toshi let out a string of expletives. "She was a negligent mother who wants people to feel sorry for her. And you are her latest chump."

Mas wasn't going to take this insult lying down. "You the one who tell a lie. You said nothing about knowing the boy."

Toshi became still, as if he were contemplating his next move. His face softened a bit as he moistened his lips. "Listen, I'm trying to cheer him up. It's better if you leave." Hideki was making his way back to where they were sitting. "I'll see you back at Ino. We can talk more then."

Mas didn't even grunt goodbye. He was being pushed aside, and he was more than willing to comply. He went around the room to exit. It was rude not to say anything to the grieving father, but he figured that Toshi could come up with a good story. He seemed skilled in telling lies.

The sky had darkened, and he glanced at his watch and calculated. It was past eight. There would be no ferries that would take him back to Ino. Why hadn't Toshi warned him, Mas first thought, and then came to the conclusion that the Senbazuru administrator really didn't care about him.

Neon signs were on full blast, an effort to make the street look happy. A couple of red-faced men in suits—early starters, obviously—stumbled through the intersection, avoiding slow-moving cars. Mas would have to find some kind of hotel to spend the night. Luckily, he'd seen some side streets with garish signs advertising "capsule hotel" for about fifty dollars a night.

"Top or bottom?" The hotel clerk asked, and when Mas failed to answer, he repeated himself, only louder.

It turned out the capsules were coffin-like accommodations, literally stacked one atop another. He was given a towel for the shared bathroom and shower and a key for a locker. Since he didn't have any bags or luggage, there was no need for that.

Mas was happy that he said, "Bottom," as it was not as difficult to climb into his capsule. The space was actually high enough for him to sit up, and it even came with cheap cotton pajamas to change into. And the capsule was air-conditioned.

Closing the curtains to his compartment, he turned off the light. Lying in such tight quarters, Mas felt like he'd been launched into space, untethered and disconnected. Haruo was dead. So were Mas's parents and brothers and sisters. Nothing was left for him in Japan, other than nephews and nieces who were barely aware of his existence. Old friends like Akemi Haneda were gone, and her relative, a journalist, was now working in a newspaper bureau in Australia. Hiroshima had once been his stomping grounds, but everything had been stripped away, leaving him utterly alone.

Chapter Five

Surprisingly, Mas slept like a baby in his crypt of a bed. He didn't know if it was because he was so exhausted from jet lag and traipsing around Hiroshima the day before. It also could have been that his body and soul were seeking repair after finding Sora's body floating in the bay. Whatever the reason, he was grateful. For the first time in a long time, he felt hopeful.

It was about nine in the morning and Mas, as best he could, pulled himself out of his capsule, dragging his clothing and towel behind him. Other men were emerging, hungover and showing the shadows of whiskers above their mouths and on their chins. All of them were wearing the same thin pajamas that the hotel had provided. One size fits all.

He did as the others did and slid on what felt like cardboard slippers and followed a few men into the communal bathroom down the hall. There was a line of shower stalls, and he went into the first available one. Afterward, all dried off and changed back into his street clothes, he found an available sink with a basket of toiletries—a cheap toothbrush with maybe two lines of bristles, a mini toothpaste the size of his pinkie, a plastic comb, and a disposable razor. In a matter of minutes, he was ready for what the day would bring.

Outside, Mas let his body memory carry him. At the intersection where Hirataya-*cho*, the street of his past, should have been, Mas saw signs for Hondori. Yah, Mas murmured. Indeed, it was the same street. He entered an expansive covered walkway, room for vehicles but meant just for pedestrians. There were quite a few people walking back and forth but not enough to bump into anyone. He took a few quick breaths and slowed down his gait. Between this and the garden, he felt more at peace. He was shielded from the elements, the blazing sun, and the occasional raindrops. He passed coffee shops, clothing stores, and even a pet store. From his grandson, Takeo, he was familiar with manga and anime. He looked for any storefronts displaying cartoon characters. And finally, there it was: a narrow space with a display case and aisle stacked with plastic monsters, dolls, and other nonsense that cost parents an arm and a leg.

A chubby man wearing a black T-shirt a size too small was behind the counter. Mas circled the skinny space once, noting a back area with a couple of video consoles where a boy sat and played.

Finally mustering enough courage, Mas approached the clerk. "Do you know Sora Tani?"

The middle-aged man was wearing thick, round, black-framed glasses. He looked as though he could be on a cartoon show himself. "Sora-*kun* used to go to school with my son." He narrowed his eyes. "Why do you ask?"

Mas wondered if the news of Sora Tani's death had hit the local newspaper. If it did, he was sunk, but he had to take a chance.

"He's my grandson," Mas lied. "His birthday is coming. I want to buy him something. Perhaps you would know."

"Hmmm," the store owner pondered. "I wouldn't know."

"When you see him last?"

"*Saa*—" the man said, taking time to think. "I guess around the time he stopped going to school. Maybe a year ago. My son might know what Sora-*kun* would want. "Kaito," he called out to the boy in the back on the video console.

No response. "Kaito!" he yelled.

"Yes!" Finally, a high-pitched response.

"Come here. Sora-*kun*'s grandfather wants to know what kind of present he should buy him."

A skinny, anemic boy appeared, wearing tinted glasses and wristbands. "I thought Sora-*kun* wasn't supposed to get any more video games. His mother banned it."

"Ah, but I'm grandpa." Mas tried the only excuse that could possibly make sense. "Grandpa can break the rules."

The boy, Kaito, frowned and pondered silently. "Well, he really loves Minecraft."

His father smiled widely, revealing a gap between his front teeth. "PlayStation, right?"

Mas waited and after the boy nodded, he nodded, too.

"Yes, I would like to buy that one."

The owner left, explaining that he needed to get the game from the back room.

Mas was now alone with the boy.

"Sora never talked about having grandparents." His closed fists were on his hips. "Except for a grandma who got sick and died last year."

This bamboo shoot of a boy was smart; there was no denying that. Before Mas could respond, he glanced at the front of the store and noticed a couple of black uniforms. The police were paying the store a visit.

"Ah, I come right back," Mas said and quickly walked down to the far end of the store, hidden by the wall of cartoon-related products.

As the police officers advanced into the stuffed store, Mas snuck out. *I understood the investigation was over*, he thought. *Isn't that what Thea said?* It had been ruled a suicide. Perhaps her sources were wrong. Or maybe the police were here for something else entirely—but that was highly unlikely, especially since Mas recognized one of them as the videographer who'd taped his interview back on the island. What would Kaito reveal to him, and how would he describe Mas? Old man, thinning gray hair. That would apply to a good number of men walking down Hondori. But then he noticed a security camera near the ceiling. *Sonofagun*, he silently cursed. Perhaps he wouldn't be as anonymous as he thought he'd be.

He was at least able to cross back onto Hondori without being stopped. This whole solo expedition had been a big disappointment. He wasn't able to see the old woman, and now the police had probably been notified of his meddling. He didn't have Haruo's ashes, and now he was involving himself in the murder investigation of a complete stranger.

There were no ferries going to the east side of the island at this time, so he had to take the same boat that he and Thea had traveled in to the west side. Drivers in their cars lined up in front of the ferry landing, waiting for passengers to debark. Mas was one of the few who got on board after the incoming passengers got off.

The ferry's passenger area was virtually empty. Carrying a plastic bag with random purchases from a nearby *konbini*, Mas took his seat in the back like the last time. As the ferry eventually began to move, he turned on his camera and pulled his reading glasses from his shirt pocket. He studied the images of Sora and the village boy. He counted the rows in front of them and then found the approximate place that they'd been sitting. He sat there, too, imagining what the boy had been thinking about.

His parents were divorced. He hated water, yet was on this boat by himself. And he had come here in May, a couple of months earlier. And what was his relationship with the boys in the village? Perhaps they'd met when his father was doing some kind of work there.

Mas gazed out the window at the expanse of the sea. On the surface, it looked so placid, almost idyllic. But underneath, a giant squid might be tearing into a Pacific saury with its horny beak, or perhaps a great white shark was chasing a finless porpoise. Nature had no mercy, and as he had thought in the past, man was no different.

He crossed his arms, sat back in the seat, and closed his eyes, attempting to imagine what Sora might have been feeling. Nothing. It was impossible. The boy was a stranger and of a different generation. What was Mas doing when he was about fourteen? The war with America was on at full blast and school was suspended. He and his classmates had little idea what all of this meant, only that food was getting scarce and their tummies rumbled with hunger more days than not.

Yet it was crucial to belong, especially at a time of war. He remembered the shock of discovering that he was a pure US citizen, a hundred percent, none of this dual citizenship status that his older siblings had. At the time of this discovery, Mas cursed his parents for forgetting to register him as a Japanese citizen. As the middle child, he was often forgotten. And now his family had made him an enemy not on purpose, but through neglect. This was a secret that only a very few knew at the time.

He took a deep breath and sat up. Thinking about the past wouldn't help the dead boy today. Then his eyes focused on something etched on the base of the seat in front of him. The Japanese would never allow any kind of graffiti to last very long after discovery, so this must have occurred recently. He pulled down his reading glasses from his head and perched them on his nose. It looked like hiragana writing that had been scratched out, maybe from the grooves of a coin. He snapped a few photos. Maybe afterward, in the right light, he could figure it out.

Once the ferry had docked and the vehicles had driven out, Mas walked onshore. It was a bit overcast—still humid, of course, but not as hot as the other days. He was walking right past the concrete *toro* when he felt his shopping bag ripped from his hands. He saw it carried on one of a line of bicycles speeding past him, disappearing into one of the narrow alleys of the village.

"*Chikusho*." Mas cursed out loud. He knew who the culprits were, and he wasn't going to let them get away with it.

He knew he shouldn't be running at his age, but he was anyhow. His whole body pulsated and his old bones rattled like a car that was being revved up after sitting in a driveway for too long.

It wasn't that difficult to find them. They were about five houses away at the intersection of another tiny alley. Above them was a blue sign with an arrow pointing to the mini Mount Fuji.

The sturdy-looking boy who'd been in the photograph with Sora on the ferry held up Mas's bag. His head was shaved, accentuating the fullness of his cheeks. "Old man, what are you doing over here?" he asked.

"Hand that over." Mas was dead serious. He wasn't afraid of these urchins.

The boys sensed his foreignness and began to mimic his American accent.

"You a gaijin, right? Because you certainly stink."

Yes, indeed, he was a foreigner, but an outsider who was also an insider. These island boys may not understand the subtleties. Mas could use their provincialism to his advantage.

"You the one who was talking to Sora." Mas pointed to the ringleader. "I saw you on the ferry."

For a moment, the boys froze in place with their bicycles. There were four of them: the ringleader, another who was tall and reedy, another with big, almost regretful eyes, and lastly, the *chibi*, the little one who had been upset about the removal of his baseball cap. Close up, his sunburnt face was filled with freckles, little ants swarming an anthill.

"You don't know us. You don't know what you saw," the ringleader finally said in a tone that lacked his previous confidence.

"Why don't you get out of Ino," the skinny one said.

Again, Mas refused to be intimidated. "I see you booger snots that are up to no good."

Mas's insult electrified the boys. The littlest one let go of his bike and went to collect something from the ground. He hurled a handful of pebbles Mas's way. They pitifully landed about a foot away from him. Mas couldn't help but laugh.

The *chibi*'s bottom lip was trembling. "*Shi-ne*," he called out. *Die*.

The skinny one repeated it, and then the ringleader. "*Shi-ne. Shi-ne*," they chanted together. The boy with the mournful eyes was the only one who stood still and said nothing.

Soon Mas was being pelted with stones of various sizes. He raised his right arm to shield his face. One especially heavy rock with a sharp edge struck his lower back and he staggered forward in pain.

"*Kora!*" a male voice shouted. It was Gohata, brandishing a walking stick like a samurai sword. "Get out of here, you twerps! Do your mischief somewhere else!"

Gohata had sway with the boys, because they immediately stopped and ran into various alleyways.

"You okay?" he asked Mas, who winced as he bent down to pick up his bag of sundries. No bones were broken, but if the district manager hadn't stepped in, he might not still be standing.

"You pretty good with that stick."

"Ah, years of kendo. That's what these boys should do. Get involved in martial arts or sports. It's their summer break and they don't know what to do with themselves. But they are sons of fishermen, all good boys. Really."

Mas remained unconvinced. Even more than the rocks, he was concerned with their jeers. Yelling "*shi-ne*" in unison like that was something that didn't happen out of the blue. They had done it before.

"I'm going to the nursing home. Do you want a ride?" Gohata asked.

"On your bike?"

"I have an extra helmet."

Mas walked with Gohata through the skinny alleys of the town to a two-story building on the side of the hill. It was apparently the largest residence in the village, with a satellite dish proudly affixed to its balcony.

"I've seen this house before," Mas said. "From the boat."

Gohata's face flushed with pride. The house was nothing

special, especially by LA standards. Apparently for the district representative, it was a palace.

Gohata put away his walking stick, and after excusing himself for a few minutes, went into the house to retrieve some things.

As he waited, Mas gazed at Gohata's garden. While his neighbors on the hill had jungles for yards, Gohata's was well manicured, with a walkway of different sized rocks fitted together. There was a vegetable garden on one side, filled with Japanese eggplant, cucumbers, and tomatoes, many of the same vegetables Chizuko had grown in their backyard in Altadena.

When Gohata finally appeared at his door with two helmets, Mas commented on the landscaping. No reaction. Obviously the front yard didn't mean much to him.

He handed Mas one of the helmets. "You're lucky that you bumped into me," he said. "It's not like we have regular taxis to transport outside visitors."

Mas pulled on the helmet and snapped on the chin strap. He detested people who complimented themselves, but he had to admit that it would have been quite an ordeal to return to the other side of the island.

Gohata swung his right leg over the seat of his motorbike, and then told Mas to get on behind him. Mas felt like a fool hanging onto Gohata's waist but if he didn't, he was bound to fall off. The district representative was good at maneuvering his motorbike; he eased into the curves of the road like a professional. He must have traveled those roads for decades.

At the T in the road by the elementary school, a white tent shaded rows of folding chairs. Colorful *kazari* decorations, normally left at gravesites during the *Obon* season, were secured on a fence by the tent. The hot breeze blew through the streamers of the *kazari*, making the scene seem festive, but it was apparently anything but.

"Our atomic-bomb commemoration. It's on Tuesday morning." Gohata turned back toward Mas, who grunted in response, remembering what Tatsuo had told him earlier.

They had putt-putted a few more miles when they caught up to someone walking by the side of the road with an open umbrella. Gohata, who seemed to pride himself on knowing everyone, slowed down. To Mas's surprise, it was Sora's mother, Rei.

"Stoppu," Mas called out.

Gohata followed Mas's command and waited. "You know her? She's the child's mother, yes?" he murmured.

Sliding off the seat, Mas unsnapped the strap of the helmet and told Gohata to leave him here with Rei. Gohata hesitated but finally took the helmet, which he hung from the motorbike's handle.

"Good afternoon," Gohata said to Rei. "I am the district representative here. At your disposal. Gohata."

Rei bowed back. "I am Tani Rei. I am Sora's mother." Her face was free of the heavy makeup she'd been wearing the day before. Without it, she looked younger and more innocent.

Gohata removed his helmet, too. "I am sorry for what has happened." For a moment, he actually seemed remorseful.

Rei again bowed, her eyes becoming cloudy with tears.

"Well, I need to attend to my family," Gohata said.

"Of course." Another bow.

The district representative put on his helmet and zoomed away.

"You still here," Mas said to Rei.

"I decided not to leave just yet. Stayed at the inn last night. It was surprisingly restful. I felt as though Sora was there, close to me."

Mas felt an ache of sadness. He had sometimes felt like that when he was on Chizuko's side of the bed after she had died.

"The villagers are kind, terribly kind. Not like anything Hideki or Toshi-*kun* described them to be."

"You know Toshi-*san*."

"Those two grew up together here. At the Children's Home, in fact."

Mas said nothing about encountering both of them in Nagarekawa-*dori*. "I went to your apartment yesterday."

"Oh, you did?" Rei's voice became high-pitched and tentative.

"Your apartment manager was looking for you. You are going to move out, he said."

"Yes, it's time to make a change. Especially now. Besides, it wasn't like Hideki was going to help me with rent. He can barely afford his own six-mat room unit."

An apartment the size of six tatami mats was indeed small, the size of Mas's room at the nursing home.

"That was our main argument during our marriage.

Money. Hideki could never hang onto a permanent job. We got married pretty young, barely in our twenties. We had a rough time of it. And then Sora was born. It was supposed to make things better. . . ."

And obviously that plan didn't work.

"Hideki even talked about moving to Ino, can you believe it? Like there would be something for him here. He loves the ocean. But not Sora." Rei stopped in her tracks and looked out at the shore. "I'll never forgive him for bringing Sora here during Golden Week. Toshi-*kun* had found him a temporary job. Hideki had Sora for a weekend and brought him here. He thought it would help our son. Of course, it was just the opposite. Sora freaked out the first night and begged to come home. I wish Toshi-*kun* would just stay out of our lives."

Just then a tabby leapt in their path and disappeared into a growth of tall grasses.

"Haruo!" Mas called out. He took out a small can of cat food from his plastic bag and popped the tabbed lid open. He clicked his tongue. "Haruo," he called out again.

The smell of the food must have enticed the cat, because it tentatively appeared in between some blades of grass. "C'mon," Mas said in English. "Food."

The cat, in its jerky fashion, approached and began devouring the can's contents.

"That's about the most miserable animal I've ever seen." Rei smiled, revealing huge eyeteeth that appeared high on the gums. "And you have a name for him, too."

Mas grunted.

"Haruo, that doesn't seem like a very cat-like name." She bent down and examined its backside by the tail. "And I'm sorry to tell you that Haruo is a girl."

"Really." Mas scratched his head.

"But Haruo. I suppose it could be a female name. That's what's popular these days, to name girls with boys' names."

After Haruo finished, she yawned and walked beside them for a while before she got bored and chased after a noise in some bushes.

When they reached the front of the nursing home, Mas noticed that Gohata's motorbike was parked outside. Still clutching onto her umbrella, Rei bowed her goodbye. "I'm continuing on to Senbazuru. Thought I'd pay Toshi-*kun* a surprise visit."

That's not such a good idea, Mas thought. But who was he to interfere?

"Where have you been?" Thea asked once Mas was inside. She was wearing her work clothes, a white polo shirt with the name of the Hiroshima senior facility embroidered on her sleeve.

Before Mas could answer, she continued, "Mukai-*san* hasn't been well."

"What happen?"

"Some kind of gastrointestinal problem," she said. "It's been such a hectic day."

Walking in the corridor away from them was Gohata

and his mother-in-law, the thieving old lady, Kondo-*Obasan*. Mas's eyes grew big and he couldn't help but to stare. "Sheezu back."

Thea nodded. "Kondo-*Obasan* was so unhappy in Hiroshima. She said she need to see the ocean or she wouldn't feel right. She kept calling her son-in-law to bring her back here." The girl focused her attention on Mas. "And you. I heard you'd gone missing. I was afraid you'd fallen into the ocean or something."

Was she really that worried?

"What happened to your clothes?"

Mas looked down to see dirt splotches from the rain of stones. "Nuttin'," he said.

"Anyway," she said, taking out her phone, "I need to get back to Hiroshima."

They said their goodbyes. There was no talk about Haruo's ashes, because it seemed inconsequential at that particular moment.

Mas returned to his room, relishing the time to be alone. He took off his clothes, emptied his plastic *konbini* bag, and stuffed it with his dirty laundry. He changed into a fresh T-shirt and pants and sat on the tatami floor, where he studied the images on his camera. It was difficult to make out exactly, but finally in the right light, Mas understood what had been scratched on the back of the chair on the ferry. The hiragana characters: *shi-ne*. Die. Did the village boys do that? And did Sora then scratch it out?

He pulled out the futon and while lying there, snacked on some red-bean pastries he'd purchased in Hiroshima.

Sleep came swiftly again; he must have been dozing for maybe an hour when he heard someone knocking on his door. *Kondo-Obasan again?* he feared. He staggered to his feet and slid open the door about an inch, wide enough for one eye. Instead of her haunted countenance, he saw a head of hair that almost looked platinum white underneath the fluorescent lights.

"Can I stay with you, *Ojisan?*" Rei asked. Her voice wavered, and the words came out in fragments.

How would that look? To share a room with a girl one-third of his age?

Mas opened the door wider. Rei's right hand was wrapped in a towel, the kind the nursing home had.

"I've done a dirty thing," she said, forcing her way in.

And before Mas could find out more information, she curled herself up on the tatami floor and fell asleep.

Chapter Six

Whens Mas woke up, there was no girl on the tatami floor. But there was a note. He wasn't sure where she got the paper, but there it was—folded origami-style into a neat envelope with "MR. ARAI" written in capital letters.

Inside, the message was in Japanese, again written all in hiragana like for an elementary school student. The note thanked him for allowing her a place to rest, and said she was on her way back to her apartment in Hiroshima. "*Arigato* for listening to my stories," she wrote. "Thank you for your kindness." Her mother had died last year, and there were few people she could really talk to.

"Sometimes strangers become friends during dark times," she ended the note. "I will never forget when you became my friend."

Mas was stunned by her vulnerability and gratitude. No one in his life—not Mari, not Chizuko, not even Genessee and Haruo—had ever thanked him like this. Mostly because he had never done anything worth thanking.

He was worried about Rei. Where would she go now? And what was this dirty thing that she had done last night?

When he stood up, he felt a sharp pain in his back. Those good-for-nothing boys had aggravated an old injury he had sustained more than fifteen years ago. Next time he was at the *konbini*, he would have to pick up some Salonpas, the menthol pads of relief.

He plodded over to the sink to wash his face. On the metal counter was a soaked towel, most likely the one that Rei had wrapped around her hand. Judging from the wet basin, the towel had been thoroughly cleaned, except for a red spot on the very corner of it. Mas had gone through enough gardening accidents to know what that redness was from. Blood.

He quickly changed into his street clothes and went to the front desk. Tatsuo had not yet returned and another clerk, younger and even more nondescript, was there to answer Mas's questions. "She said that she was your daughter—she is, isn't she?" The young man showed no outward expression of anxiety, but he began speaking faster, making it difficult for Mas to understand him. "It was okay that I let her in, right? She said that she'd fallen and hurt her hand, so I gave her a towel."

Mas merely grunted, failing to reassure the young man. He switched to the outdoor slippers at the *genkan*, the recessed entryway, and as soon as he arrived in front of the glass automatic doors, they whooshed open, the familiar, oppressive heat hitting his face. Where did she go? Most likely back to the inn, he guessed. There, what was that on the ground? Not scarlet petals of a tropical flower but drops of blood trailing from the north.

He followed the drops down the concrete road, past a few oyster factories, the jetty, and then the ferry landing, north toward the overgrown green hills of the island. He finally reached a fenced campus with a playground and gray two-story buildings in the distance. A rock statue of an origami crane with an accompanying vertical sign reading, "SENBAZURU" was set into a platform of tiny rocks next to a dark wood building. Mas approached the doorway and pressed his face against the glass. Based on the reception counter and desks behind it, this was obviously the school office. He jiggled the doorknob and checked his watch. It was too early for it to be open.

Behind the office was a small detached house. Rei's closed umbrella, most likely forgotten, was leaning by the door frame.

Mas banged on the door. He heard some kind of movement inside, faint and unsteady. He banged again.

Finally the door swung open, revealing a shirtless Toshi. He had a bit of a farmer's tan, dark arms and a chest as pale and smooth as a baby's behind.

"Ah, Arai-*san*, what is wrong—"

Mas pushed his way into the principal's modest home. He didn't bother to take off his shoes. He wanted to be fully gaijin in this moment.

"Is she here?"

Toshi's mouth remained open for a moment. "Who?"

"Tani Rei. She told me that she was coming yesterday

afternoon. And then in the middle of night, I see her again. She was hurt."

Toshi sat down at his kitchen table and exhaled. "Please, Arai-*san*, sit down. I will explain everything to you."

Mas first resisted Toshi's invitation. He was certainly being more hospitable than at the encounter at the hostess bar, but he was still untrustworthy. But Mas was here for answers, and the only way to get them was to sit at the table.

Toshi took a deep breath and dove in. "Yes, she came yesterday. I was in the middle of a meeting with my teachers when I was summoned to the office. Embarrassing, to say the least. I didn't know why she was here." Toshi picked up a pack of cigarettes that was on the table next to a bottle of whiskey. It certainly seemed like it had been one of those nights. He offered a cigarette to Mas, who declined, reluctantly. After lighting one for himself, Toshi continued. "We never got along. Even when Hideki started going around with her. I didn't think they made a good fit. Hideki needed a happy, strong person. Not someone so sensitive and needy."

Toshi blew out some smoke and tapped the end of the cigarette into an ashtray. He left the burning cigarette on the edge of the ashtray and started pacing around his kitchen, avoiding some broken shards of glass that had been swept into the corner.

"Yesterday, she came over to tell me that it was all my fault. Sora's death. That I should never have made arrangements for Hideki to work here in May. That nothing good could come out of this island."

"She lost her son." Mas said it not as an excuse but as a fact. What happened to the grace he extended to his friend, Hideki? The same if not more should apply to the mother.

The bedroom door opened, startling Mas for a moment. "It was unbelievable," said Thea. "She was just awful. She called Toshi a 'boy killer.' " Her long, dark hair was tousled and loosely tied back in a ponytail. She had dark smudges underneath her eyes, probably due to her makeup being mussed up in her sleep. She was wearing an oversized T-shirt with the message, "HIROSHIMA CARP," the region's professional baseball team. It was clear to Mas: she had stayed the night in Toshi's bedroom. And based on how they both looked, the relationship was far from platonic.

Mas honestly didn't care what these young people did in their private lives. "Is that why you hit her?" he asked Toshi, referring to Rei's hand injury and the glass on the floor.

"Of course not. I would never hit a woman."

"She was bleeding."

Toshi sat back in his chair and poured himself some whiskey, a tonic for breakfast.

"It was me," Thea said. "I threw a glass at the wall to make her stop saying such awful things. And no, I didn't hit her. She went to pick it up and she cut herself. She ran away before I could treat the wound." She twisted her arms together and leaned against the door frame. She looked both so young and so old at the same time. "I'm sorry Arai-*san*. I know this all may be a shock."

Mas didn't respond. This whole time he had imagined Thea to be one kind of person, and she was actually two.

A cell phone on the table began to both vibrate and ring. "Ah, I have to get ready for work," Toshi announced, going back into the bedroom. A few minutes later he emerged with an armful of clothing and disappeared through a door opposite the kitchen. Soon they heard the hum of water traveling through pipes.

Mas awkwardly remained in his chair. He should go, but he was still a bit shaken from all that he had just discovered.

"Let me at least make you breakfast, Arai-*san*," Thea offered. "Hot coffee?"

How could Mas refuse?

After not only coffee, but scrambled eggs and thick toasted Japanese bread with ample amounts of butter, they finally began to talk again.

"How long dis goin' on?"

Thea covered her mouth as she chewed her last corner of bread. "About nine months. We met on a ferry ride."

Of course, Mas thought. The ferry.

"He's a good man. He devotes himself to the children here."

Even Mas had to admit that it was commendable that a vibrant young man was committing his life to help abandoned children.

She began to clear the table of the dirty dishes. Before taking Mas's, she said, "Listen, I do have a request. You're not going to tell Mukai-*san* about us, are you? She's actually my sponsor here. She'll tell my mother, and my parents will probably tell me to return to the Philippines."

This mess was her business, and Mas had no desire to

spill the beans. What was it to him whether or not she was having a relationship with the Children's Home director? He shook his head. He would say nothing.

Toshi, perhaps his ears burning from this topic of conversation, appeared from the bathroom looking somewhat respectable in a suit and tie. "*Saa*—," he said, indicating that he was ready to go. "I will be off." Thankfully, he and Thea refrained from any public displays of affection, but based on the look they exchanged, the couple seemed serious. Mas stretched out his fingers in a weak wave of goodbye. Message received. The two men weren't friends and probably wouldn't be in the future, either. But for now, they could exchange basic pleasantries.

The door opened and closed. "I'zu leave Japan soon," Mas informed Thea. "Need to go home."

The girl nodded. She seemed relieved that her secrets would remain on the island.

Mas took his exit, picking up the collapsed umbrella on the porch. He doubted that Rei would return here again. Walking back to the office, he noticed a small gate that had been left ajar. As there was a lock on it, the door was meant to be closed to outsiders. Perhaps Toshi had accidentally left it open in his rush to go to his meeting? Mas was curious to see the residents of Senbazuru, at least from a distance.

The gate opened onto a dirt baseball diamond. In the early morning hush, he heard the ring of an aluminum bat making contact with a ball. Two boys dressed in shorts and T-shirts were on the diamond practicing pitching and hitting. Mas picked up about five of the balls that had landed in the outfield and walked them to the pitcher's mound.

"Ah, *domo*," the pitcher thanked Mas.

"Are you looking for Ikeda-*sensei*?" The batter approached the mound. He was slightly older than the pitcher. Maybe about fifteen.

"I was just with him," Mas explained.

"Relative?" asked the pitcher.

Mas chose not to answer the question directly. "I am from America."

"America?" The two boys' interest was immediately piqued. "Where?"

"Los Angeles," Mas replied. "Rosu." No Japanese would know where Altadena was.

"Rosu! *Sugoi!*" Again the two baseball players seemed delighted to meet someone from overseas.

"That is my dream to go to Rosu. Dodgers, right?" the pitcher said.

Mas nodded. "Actually my—" he had forgotten how to say son-in-law in Japanese, so he just substituted son for it—"my son works for the Dodgers. He takes care of the grass."

"Hehhhhhh. *Sugoi*," the boys said in unison. They certainly seemed easily impressed.

"I heard that baseball players can join the pros right from high school," the batter interjected.

It was true, but they still had to go through the farm teams and prove themselves. Mas tried to explain it to the boys, but somehow he couldn't find the words.

They didn't seem bothered by his limited Japanese.

"I heard in America that you can do something wrong, but they won't hold it against you." The batter was definitely an observer of American culture.

"Second chance, right?" the other one added.

The boys' faces, free of blemishes and scars, held so much optimism that it was breaking Mas's heart. For their sake, he took his time in answering. He thought of all the times that he was not given a second chance, just cast aside and ignored. He had to find his own ways to reinvent himself and it had not been easy. He answered as honestly as he could. "Yes, it can happen."

"Yes, America," both of them said joyously as they returned to their positions.

Mas returned to the gate and closed it behind him firmly to make sure that no other outsiders would make their way in.

When Mas returned to the nursing home, the older detective with the hedgehog hair was sitting in the lobby by himself. Mas considered staying outside and hiding in the trees in the back, but what purpose would that serve? It was getting hotter than hell out there, and if the detective wanted to skin his hide, he'd get it sooner or later.

Making sure to leave Rei's umbrella outside, he entered the building, causing the detective to immediately rise. *Sonofagun*, Mas said to himself. *I was right. This guy's coming for me.*

"Hello, Arai-*san*, I need a moment of your time."

Mas swallowed the spit that had accumulated in the back of his throat. They both took a seat in the lobby. Nobody was visible in the office, and Mas was glad to have at least some degree of privacy.

"We heard you were at a game and manga shop in Hondori. And you were asking questions about Tani Sora."

Mas nodded, his heart racing. "He had a friend there. At least that's what I heard."

"Why did you feel that you had to interfere in our investigation? I know that you are a gaijin, but that is highly irregular here in Japan."

Mas's hands began to shake; he sat on them so that his nervousness wouldn't be so obvious. The tone of the detective's voice reminded him of the military police who had hounded him and his childhood friends like him: Kibei Nisei, born in America but raised in Japan. "I didn't know you were still looking into Sora's death."

"The case is not yet closed, Arai-*san*. In fact, it's very much open."

Mas lowered his head as if to apologize.

"And the director of Senbazuru, Ikeda Toshi. How well do you know him?"

Mas considered the detective's question. Why was he asking about Toshi? "I don't know him," he said. "I mean, I met him when the body was found."

"Do you remember his response?"

"Well, he didn't know the dead boy."

"Don't you think that's strange, since he's the son of one

of his closest friends?"

That had bothered Mas, of course, but he didn't express it.

"Do you have any more information to share with me, then?"

Mas got up. "Please come with me."

The detective followed Mas down the corridor, past the open doors of the residents. A few pulled themselves up from their beds, curious about the presence of the detective who walked with such confidence and brashness. Walking with him, Mas almost felt like he was a delinquent boy awaiting his punishment. When they passed Ayako's door, Mas made sure that his eyes were focused on what was ahead of him. He didn't need to be interrogated by her, too.

They entered his room and Mas was glad that he had made sure to fold the futons and put them to the side. And Rei's note was safely out of sight in the depths of his suitcase.

The detective sat on his legs on the tatami floor. It was judo-style, and even though he was probably in his fifties, his body was still supple. *Why should that surprise you*, Mas thought. *Here is a man who catches criminals for a living.*

"I never gave you my *meishi*. Suzuki Goro." The policeman pulled out a case from his pocket, opened it, and took out an immaculate business card. Barely bending his neck forward, he presented it to Mas with both hands. Mas was Japanese enough to bow his head deeply, his forehead almost touching the tatami floor. Of course, he didn't have a business card to exchange. His last one, which boasted "ORIENTAL GARDENING," had been printed maybe four decades earlier.

Mas brought out the camera and attempted to find the photo he had taken. He kept pressing the button to advance the images and then had to go back. He had to stop to get his reading glasses and then started all over again. Finally he located the photo with the boy. "I didn't know that I had taken this," he explained. "It's Sora with a village boy."

There seemed to be some kind of recognition in Suzuki's eyes, but he revealed nothing.

Mas took back the camera and found the picture of the message that had been carved in the seat in the ferry.

The detective stared at it for a while, "*Shi-ne*," he said, and Mas nodded.

"I'm going to have to borrow this camera. I will return it after we have downloaded those photos."

Mas didn't care. Bringing the camera wasn't his idea, anyway.

"Arai-*san*, I don't know how it is in America, but we are having an epidemic of bullying here in Japan. It wouldn't surprise me if Sora-*kun* was being targeted." Suzuki moved his position so he was sitting cross-legged. Even he had a breaking point in terms of sitting on his legs. "But that doesn't mean he was coerced into committing suicide by the boys."

Mas knew that. He sat cross-legged, too, and faced the detective.

"Did the mother tell you where she was that night?"

Mas shook his head. He'd assumed she had a night job.

"She has not yet come up with an adequate alibi for us. Do you think that is what a proper mother does? Stays out all night while her *hikokomori* son is by himself?"

Mas kept his eyes on the tatami and studied its seams. They were actually not completely straight.

"I don't know if she asked you to look into her son's death, but I want to tell you to stop. This is the police's job, and we are quite capable of handling it."

Mas bowed his head.

"By the way, do you know where she went? She left the inn without paying for her additional last days of stay. And none of the ferrymen recall transporting her back to Ujina."

"No," Mas said, feeling the heat rise to his head. Did Suzuki know that she had spent the night here in his room on practically the same spot that he was sitting on? That needed to remain a secret; it would be too difficult to explain their relationship.

The detective stood up effortlessly, without even using his hands for balance. "Oh, and I may be seeing you again, Arai-*san*. I'll be staying here in the home until tomorrow, for the atomic-bomb commemoration. I figure that I should stay around to make sure everything goes smoothly."

"I'm not planning to go," Mas informed him.

"I hope you won't be sneaking away." Mas couldn't tell if Suzuki was joking. "I expect to be fully informed on your whereabouts and when you leave Hiroshima."

I'm no prisoner, Mas thought. But maybe he was.

Before the detective left, he turned from the sliding door. "You were carrying an umbrella when you were walking to the nursing home. That umbrella sure looked like the one that Tani-*san* had been carrying."

Mas stayed in his room for a while, almost afraid to breathe too loudly. His movements were being scrutinized from within the nursing home. He glanced at his watch, which read 9 p.m. Los Angeles time. If only he could hear Genessee's voice, he could be set right again.

Workers were pushing carts of food down the hallway, and Mas took the opportunity during all this activity to slip away to the office. As soon as he saw Tatsuo in the office, he felt a sense of relief. He waved at him through the glass window, and Tatsuo rushed to open the door for him.

"Arai-*san*, how have you been? Makoto-*san* mentioned something about your daughter coming to visit."

Makoto must have been the name of the young man who had been working there earlier.

"I need to call America," Mas announced, and Tatsuo was only too happy to comply.

Mas gripped the telephone receiver in the same office where he had been interrogated. A dial tone and then the familiar voice. "Hello."

"Hallo."

"Mas." As soon as Genessee spoke his name, he felt a wave of relief. "How are you?"

"Not too good." He couldn't fake his feelings. Slowly, in dribs and drabs, he told his wife almost everything that had transpired: The discovery of the boy's body in the ocean.

The bullying village boys. The police investigation. He did leave out the part about the young mother staying overnight in his room.

"My goodness. You should come home, Mas. I'm sure you can change your flight."

He fell silent. He had to confess. "I'zu lost Haruo."

"Honey, I can't hear you. What?"

"Haruo gone." Mas explained how his best friend's ashes had been stolen.

"Well, you have to tell her. The sister."

Mas knew that was what Genessee would say. "Sheezu gonna be mad."

"Well, what do they say—*shikataganai*. You can't worry about that. It's not your fault if one of the patients stole the ashes. You did what you promised Spoon—you took the ashes to that island. You can't be responsible for a theft. You didn't know anything about that place."

"How you'zu doin'?" Mas asked.

"My knee is healing up. The physical therapy is going well. Pretty soon, I'll be chasing you all around the house," Genessee said. Nothing sounded better.

After he said goodbye to Genessee, Mas took a deep breath. He knew what he needed to do, what he should have done from the get-go. To put it off a few more minutes, he sat by himself in the cell-like office with blank white walls.

Why had he agreed to this *mendokusai* expedition again? Yes, he blamed Spoon, and he also blamed another friend's widow, Lil Yamada. "Haruo was so committed to you; it would be so nice if you would do this for him," she'd said. Mas had deeply resented her guilt trip, mostly because it was so effective.

He tried not to think of his life without Haruo when he returned to Southern California. They had lived close enough that Mas had been able to go by his and Spoon's Montebello house nearly every day during hospice. Others had dropped out or else just left food on the doorstep for Spoon, but not Mas. He brought his copy of *The Rafu Shimpo*, a Japanese American newspaper published in Little Tokyo, usually a couple of days old, to their household and would start summarizing all the obituaries, Haruo's favorite activity.

Since Mas's reading ability was appalling, he would just say the name of the deceased, after which Haruo would comment, "Datsu so-and-so's brotha, *desho*?" or "Dat guy in Heart Mountain." Mas would scan the obituary and then either nod or shake his head. "Yah, you'zu right," or "nah, dat anotha guy."

When Mas arrived one day, the white mortuary van was parked in the driveway. The sight of it was a punch to the gut, and he couldn't park anywhere near it. He walked a block to the house, his whole body shaking. When he arrived at the house, Spoon called out for the workers to stop what they were doing.

"Wait. This is my husband's best friend. He needs to see him before you take him away."

Mas stumbled into the extra bedroom, where Spoon and her daughter had set up a hospital bed. But that body wasn't Haruo's. Yes, it had the same hideous scar and the patch of now completely white hair. His mouth was wide open, frozen in that state. His eyes were closed, hiding the existence of his fake eye.

"I was gone only a few minutes and I found him like this. They say that people finally feel that they can let go when no one's around."

Haruo, sumimasen, Mas apologized, *for everything. For not being there and sometimes not listening when I was there. And in Hiroshima, for losing track of where you were.*

After remembering all this for a while, he rose. He went over to thank Tatsuo, who was sitting at a desk, before going straight to that ocean-view room. It was as if Ayako had been waiting for him all along.

"*Daijobu?*" he asked from the open door. "You doin' orai?"

"Where have you been?" Ayako asked, still lying on her pillow. Her face was ashen gray, and it was obvious that she wasn't doing well. "Why are you torturing me? Why are you keeping my brother's ashes from me?"

He took a deep breath and braced himself for Ayako's reaction. "Gone. Somebody steal. I thinksu maybe Kondo-*Obasan*."

Ayako pressed a button on her bed railing, which elevated her mattress so she could sit up. "That's the most elaborate lie I've ever heard. Why would she do such a thing?"

"I dunno."

"I heard a detective from Hiroshima is staying here. If you don't hand over my brother's ashes, I will make sure you are arrested."

"But I don't—"

"I don't want to hear any excuses. The next time I see you, you better have it with you."

Mas returned to his room in the foulest mood ever. He tried to watch television to while away the time, but his mind couldn't follow any of the program's comedic antics. He began to miss the heinous daytime shows in America, in which a couple's shame was laid out bare for all to see, not for judgment but for entertainment. At least in that case, people weren't putting on masks to pretend that they were better than they really were. Their ugly motives were cut out from the bodies and paraded around for public scorn.

He didn't know what he was going to do about Ayako and the ashes. He knew the detective had more important things to do than deal with this matter. But Ayako could still make it quite unpleasant for Mas. Even if he snuck back to Altadena, he could imagine the series of international calls that Spoon would receive. He guessed that she'd have to change her phone number. And he'd have to come up with the money to reimburse her for this trip.

He had intended to make do without dinner, but it was after seven and his stomach was growling like a sick animal. No matter how terrible Ayako said the food was at the home, it was edible, right? He wandered over to the cafeteria, where workers were cleaning off plates and bowls from long tables.

"Are you closed?" Mas asked, feeling foolish. One of the cafeteria workers, his hands gloved, looked surprised to see him and went to the back to talk to another worker.

A woman wearing a mask and hairnet emerged from the back. She had on a full-length apron as if she was conducting science experiments rather than preparing food. She presented him with a tray holding a bowlful of *okayu*, rice gruel, chopsticks, and hot green tea.

The watery *okayu* was tasteless. Absolutely no salt. Just the addition of one pickled plum would have brightened the eating experience. Again *shikataganai*. Had to bear down and eat it, at least for bodily sustenance.

The windows of the cafeteria faced toward the front. A Buddhist sculpture loomed, a standing figure emerging from an open lotus blossom. Below the sculpture was a stone box, probably something to hold the remains of those who had died in the home. Strung over the windows were origami cranes, the only sign of the facility's connection to the Bomb.

Mas must have been telegraphing his displeasure with the bland mush, because the cafeteria worker returned to his table with a glass container of black strips.

"*Konbu*," she said through her mask. "For my own lunches."

He bowed his head and accepted the gift, picking up ample bunches of shiny marinated seaweed with the other end of his chopsticks. Stirred into the rice gruel, the seaweed markedly improved it, causing Mas to actually smile.

He put a little of the gruel on a napkin. A treat for Haruo, he figured. Bowing his thanks, he made his way outside. He was hoping for some solitude. Instead there was Tatsuo on the ridge, looking through a pair of binoculars.

Mas walked quietly behind him, but it wasn't quiet enough, because Tatsuo turned and gestured for him to take a look.

At first, all Mas could see through the binoculars were the oyster racks and the slow, rising tide. Tatsuo pointed to a figure in the distance. "Suzuki-*san*."

Mas readjusted the binoculars and focused the lens on the detective. He was close to the oyster farm. He had rolled up his pant legs and the water reached his calves. He seemed to be holding something round covered in fabric.

"What's he doing?" Mas said out loud, not really to Tatsuo but to himself.

"He's been leaving these balls covered in different-color T-shirts in different places in the bay. I think he's trying to figure out where the boy was when he was carried to the jetty over here."

The tides rise quickly overnight, Tatsuo explained to Mas. "Odds are the body was south of us."

"He's trying to find out where the boy was when he was killed," Mas said.

Tatsuo seemed genuinely shocked by his choice of words. "I don't think he was killed. Maybe where the 'incident' happened is a better way to put it."

Mas gritted his teeth. He didn't care for semantics. The detective wouldn't be here for a simple "incident." Whether or not the islanders believed it, this was about murder.

Chapter Seven

The next morning, Mas heard voices emanating from the hallway. Not one or two, but a series of them. There were older ones, speaking the strong Hiroshima dialect, and then younger, soft-pitched ones. They seemed on the move.

Mas pushed open the door a crack, enough to see the nursing-home workers pushing wheelchairs and assisting residents with walkers.

He glanced at his watch. The atomic-bomb ceremony was due to start in half an hour.

Dressed in a pressed suit, the detective marched behind the parade of residents and their aides like a drill sergeant. How one man could stop any trouble at the ceremony was beyond logic. But then, there was probably no trouble to be had.

All Mas knew was that he would not be there to witness anything. He wondered if Ayako felt strong enough to attend. She probably willed herself into recovery. Here was her chance to make an appearance in front of an audience beyond the nursing home, and this opportunity would not be squandered.

He took a shower and changed into his last clean set of underwear. His khaki pants were supposed to carry him throughout most of his trip and they were now on day four. He felt liberated in the half-empty nursing home. A few voices still called out in pain or for help, but as the more ambulatory ones left for the ceremony, fewer eyes were watching his activities.

Curious about the results of the detective's experiment, Mas went outside only to see a line of five balls outfitted in T-shirts of different colors—white, red, blue, yellow, and green. They were all soaking wet, a few adorned with a garland of seaweed. Where had each of them ended up? Only the detective had that privileged information.

"Mas, you haven't left yet." Thea was hurrying down the pathway in a pair of flats. She was more dressed up than usual, wearing a simple black frock. Mas could not look into the young woman's face. Their last encounter was so personal and intimate. They had broken through the necessary distance that makes interactions superficial and carefree. Thea, though, acted without any self-consciousness, which helped put Mas more at ease.

"You're going to the ceremony, aren't you? I don't want to go late by myself."

"No, I don't go." That's the last place Mas wanted to be.

"C'mon. I need to at least show my face. Toshi is going to say a few words at the end. They never ask anyone from Senbazuru to participate. Mukai-*san* was really against it, but she was overruled."

To hear that Ayako might be a bit agitated at the ceremony was certainly an enticement, but not enough to win Mas over. Reluctantly, he told Thea about his encounter with Ayako the night before. "Somebody took Haruo," Mas admitted, explaining that he believed the ashes were stolen by Kondo-*Obasan*.

"That's why you were so desperate to see her," Thea said, referring to Mas's trip to the Hiroshima facility. "I don't remember her bringing anything that looked like ashes."

"*Zannen*," Mas said in Japanese. There wasn't any English-language equivalent that he could think of. It was too bad, but he couldn't dwell on it. He needed to move on.

"You know, we were visited by that detective, Suzuki, yesterday. He stayed an hour, just questioning Toshi. He wanted to know where he was from sundown to about 10 o'clock."

Mas raised his eyebrows.

"Yes, we were together, and I confirmed it. But he spent most of the time asking about Rei. We, of course, had to tell him what happened with her. How she burst in the house, yelling bloody murder."

"You'zu really don't tell him dat."

"We did. Toshi explained how Rei was always on edge."

"Datsu no good," Mas murmured. The detective was stacking the deck against Rei. "Maybe I go to ceremony," he told Thea.

"You should. Almost everyone will be there."

The girl knew shortcuts and shady paths to get to the garden. As they walked by elderly men playing lawn ball, it was obvious that not all islanders were interested in revisiting the past.

When they finally arrived at the tent, all the folding

chairs were full with people dressed in black. Even the children were in their black-and-white uniforms, making Mas feel even more self-conscious in his khaki pants and tan striped shirt. He usually felt that he could disappear in sand-colored clothing, but here at the gloomy memorial, he stuck out like a sore thumb.

Punctuating the black were sashes of bright purple and orange worn by the priests. One of them was chanting with some true believers following along. The detective and Go-hata were seated in the front row. Someone had pulled out a chair to make room for Ayako's wheelchair. Mas was grateful that he and Thea were standing in the rear, their heads barely shaded by the roof of the tent.

Three young people—two girls and the sad-looking boy—were ushered up to the front. They took turns making an offering to the rock memorial and Buddhist scroll that was attached to the tent. Their rosaries drooping from their wrists, the girls brought flowers and a string of folded cranes, while the boy carried a green bamboo vase. The ringleader boy, *chibi,* and the skinny one were huddled together in the seats, chuckling and probably plotting an evil diversion, until a teacher went back and hushed them into silence.

All the attendees were now invited to come up to the makeshift altar and make incense offerings. Mas was glad that offerings would start from the front rows, as the Buddhist funerals he went to in Los Angeles usually started with the back. By the time he and Thea were making their offering, the attendees would be bored and restless, their minds on anything besides what was transpiring before them.

Tatsuo pushed Ayako forward in her wheelchair to be first in line. Mas was again reminded how she was completely different from her younger brother despite their physical similarities. Haruo would have never called any special attention to himself during the offering of incense. His eyes—or at least his one good eye—would have been focused on his own business and not on any other's at a time like this. Ayako, on the other hand, made it a point to survey the crowd from right to left before being rolled back to her spot. Unfortunately she and Mas locked eyes briefly, which caused her to produce a most unattractive scowl.

Mas wanted to forego his own participation, but he knew that would be impossible. He kept his eyes down on the grass and tried to think of anything else—Haruo the cat, Genessee, Takeo—as he waited his turn. Once at the urn, he dutifully pinched the incense and released it into a shallow dish. And just to make it official, he put his hands together and silently lifted up a prayer specifically for Sora and Rei.

After the incense offering was complete, Toshi began his address. Thea's face was shining, and Mas almost felt embarrassed to stand next to such a lovesick child. Who knows how long this union would last? It was only a matter of time before Ayako found out, and the result would not be good. Mas could easily picture Thea's pink nose and tears as she awaited a flight back to the Philippines from Kansai Airport.

"I want to thank you for the opportunity for Senbazuru

to participate in this ceremony," Toshi said. Mas couldn't see Ayako's face, but he noticed that her head was down, as if she were taking a nap. "As most of you know, the Children's Home was started after the war because of the Bomb, since most of their parents had been killed and there was no one to take care of these children.

"This island has since come to represent healing, whether it be for the youth or the seniors who might be *hibakusha*."

He said a few more words before completing his speech. Gohata, dressed in the same type of black suit, was up next. "As you know, the Kondo family has been longtime residents of this island, ever since the first Sino-Japanese War, in the late 1800s," he said. A noise came from the tool shed across the way. The door flung open, banging against a metal trash can.

Rei, her blond hair piled up like a bird's nest, stumbled out. Her pale skin looked sunburned, and she was wearing the same clothes that she had on the other night. She appeared badly hungover. What a change from the cool and collected woman with the umbrella he had first met on the shore. Inside, she must have been feeling how she was acting now. Mas felt afraid for her.

She stood and stared at the ceremony, as if she hadn't fully registered what was happening.

"Oh my goodness," Thea whispered. "She looks like a zombie."

Gohata continued talking, but it was obvious that he had lost most of his audience to Rei. It only got worse when

Detective Suzuki rose and made his way to the garden.

"This anniversary is a time to pursue peace," Gohata said.

Rei, spotting the detective, began to run toward the pathway by the shoreline.

"For nations to come together, not as enemies, but as friends for a better future."

The detective did not chase after her, but he did walk to the ridge to get a better look. By the time he returned to the tent, the ceremony was almost over.

The detective approached the teacher at the village school and whispered something in his ear. Based on the teacher's reaction, the message had been unpleasant, and Mas was curious what would happen next. As soon as Gohata made his closing comments, the teacher addressed his charges. "The detective has requested that we have a special meeting at the school now. All students and their parents are required to attend."

The four trouble-making boys, even the ringleader, had become oddly quiet. The skinny one looked sick to his stomach, and the one with the mournful face, who already was pale, looked even more washed out. The little one, the *chibi*, was so agitated that Mas thought he might spin out like a top.

What was the detective going to do with the village children? Had he received any new leads that implicated them in Sora's death?

Mas was happy that the detective was turning up the heat on the boys. Whether or not they had done something criminal, they were bullies. He didn't know if a session with the Hiroshima Police Department could make them change their ways, but it wouldn't hurt to try.

Thea had received some new information as well. The detective had issued a directive that the islanders must immediately report any sightings of Rei. "There won't be any way that she'll be able to get off the island," she told Mas. "She's not allowed to get on any of the ferries."

Rei was cornered, just as Mas had been in the nursing home.

"Disgraceful," Mas heard Ayako say to Thea as they boarded a van back to the facility. He held up his hand to Thea to signal that he'd see her later.

The sun was blazing, and Mas wiped the sweat off his face with the back of his hand. Cleanup crews were already stacking the folding chairs, leaving the *kazari* decorations attached to the iron fencing. There was no breeze, so the streamers remained still.

Mas crossed the street to take a look at the tool shed. The outlying garden was a naturalistic design with young seedlings and flower stalks planted here and there—small sunflowers, orange lantanas, drooping purple dahlias, and red blanket flowers. It wasn't much, but in this heat, the drought-tolerant garden was a worthy effort.

The tool shed served not only as a place to store equipment, it was also a makeshift museum. Mas shuddered to think that Rei had stayed overnight in that place. In between a lawnmower and edgers and clippers hanging from the walls were laminated black-and-white images of a line of skulls and stacks of bones. All unearthed ten years ago, they were the remains of eighty-five atomic-bomb survivors who had died on the island. In 1971, the bones of more than six hundred victims had been found on the school grounds, a reminder that the past still haunted the new generation that had nothing to do with World War II.

Also on the walls were photographs that Mas knew too well. Ravaged people, their clothes literally burned away from their bodies, desperate for help. These, too, were in black and white, while his memories were in full color.

"I hope that girl didn't deface anything in here." A raspy voice sounded behind him.

Konbini Kondo, Gohata's sister-in-law, stood outside of the shed, wearing a bonnet and apron over her black dress.

"I'm sure everything is where it's supposed to be."

Kondo took off her gardening gloves to straighten out two sunflowers in a vase on a makeshift ledge underneath images of bones discovered a few years ago. "You learning what America did to Hiroshima?"

In the growing heat, Mas was becoming impatient. "I am a *hibakusha*."

Kondo took a few steps back in the dirt as if she couldn't quite take it in. "I thought you were an American."

Again, it felt strange to be known on an island of strangers. "I am. I was born in California, but taken to Hiroshima when I was a baby. I was in Hiroshima until I was about eighteen years old."

"So you are a *hibakusha*." She wouldn't have believed it unless she said it out loud, Mas figured.

Anticipating her next question, he said, "Train station."

"*Soka*," Kondo soaked in his personal information for a few moments before she began to share hers. "My mother was walking about the Kyobashi River. She was pregnant at that time." She didn't continue, and Mas could only assume what had happened to the baby.

"*Zannen,*" he said. It was certainly sad, a waste of a life.

Kondo's lined face softened. "They didn't want to have any more babies, but then I was born. And then my sister."

Mas grunted and studied the photos on the wall of the shed.

"You've met my mother. She is staying at the home," she said.

Mas had already figured out that the pregnant mother in the story was none other than the woman who had stolen his friend's ashes.

"What is your name?" she asked.

"Arai Masao."

"Kondo Kiseki. Pleased to meet you."

They bowed to each other. Somehow Mas's status had changed from foe to friend.

"So you taking care of this garden."

Kiseki nodded.

"Hard job."

"Yes, well, it's my hobby. And someone has to do it."

Mas wasn't much about small talk, and their conversation had lost most of its steam. "I better get back to the home. I'll need to prepare to leave soon."

"Oh, yes." Kiseki was almost smiling. "Well, safe travels."

Mas bowed his goodbye. As he walked back to the

home, he couldn't help but wonder why news of his departure would make the woman so happy.

The nursing home was buzzing with gossip about what happened at the ceremony. Of course, the main subject was Rei.

"I can't believe she would run from the police like that," an old woman was saying to her companion in the lobby.

"Truly unthinkable."

"I think I saw her here a couple of nights ago."

"How could that be? You are imagining things again."

"No, I think—" Upon seeing Mas, the woman shrank in her wheelchair. Apparently Mas was also a topic of discussion today.

"Ah, Arai-*san*." Tatsuo called out from the front desk. "Suzuki-*san* had to leave to prepare the security for the big ceremony in Hiroshima. He asked me to return this to you."

He stepped back to one of the metal desks and retrieved Mas's camera next to a stack of folders. Handing it over to Mas, he asked, "They find something in there?"

"Just a child's prank." Mas had wished it had been more, but based on the detective's quick departure, he probably hadn't come up with anything substantial during his meeting with the schoolchildren.

Mas excused himself. All that sun and walking had completely worn him out; if he didn't get some kind of sustenance he would surely collapse. The cafeteria was closed, but he was able to flag down the worker who had fed him the previous day. After a trip to the kitchen, she presented Mas with a couple of rice balls and a tin of sardines, also most likely from her personal stash. With his meal in hand, he tiptoed past Ayako's open door. He didn't need to be further interrogated today.

In his room, he opened the sardine can with its attached tab instead of a key, which was standard for the old-fashioned rectangular tins. Standing over the sink, he pulled out a couple of slimy fish, put his head back like a seal and threw them in his open mouth. Chomping on them and the rice balls together was probably the best meal he'd had in Hiroshima—after the *okonomiyaki*, of course.

He was thirsty, so he went back to the vending machine in the cafeteria to buy an ice-cold green tea. As he bent down to retrieve the bottle, he both smelled and heard someone behind him. The smell was a mixture of sickness and neglect, like old used tissues forgotten in a sweater pocket. When he turned around, Kondo-*Obasan* the thief stood in front of him as if she was waiting for something, perhaps an explanation.

After hearing about her background from her daughter, Mas couldn't stay mad. He tried to walk around her, but she moved swiftly to block his path.

"They always take everything away," she said, her eyes barely visible underneath the flaps of flesh.

Mas frowned. Did he need to press the alarm button to alert the office?

"They lie. They want me to forget. But I will never forget."

Who is wanting you to forget? Mas wanted to ask. But he knew his question would probably not result in anything coherent.

"Don't listen to them," she muttered, shuffling away back to her room.

It was naptime, and Mas halfway hoped that when he woke up, all of this would have been a madcap nightmare brought on by too many helpings of jalapeño peppers. When he got up, it was the same warm tatami room with a lonely sardine in a tin next to him.

This would be a perfect treat for Haruo the cat. Taking the tin with him, Mas went outside to sit on the bench under the camphor tree. It was a truly magnificent tree, an old one judging from its branches, which stretched out like arthritic limbs. It was at least twenty feet high, the height of almost four of him. Mas respected old trees, and lately even preferred them to pruned specimens. Once the roots were established, they didn't need much care from humans to survive. And they outlived humans, enduring the topsy-turvy mess that humans created through hubris and hatred.

He sat in the shade for a good half hour, but she never appeared. He left the open tin underneath the bench. Surely this would entice Haruo to make an appearance, but still nothing. Did he make a mistake by bringing the half-blind cat to this side of the island? Perhaps Haruo, who had faced familiar bullies on the west side, would survive better back there than here on the mysterious east side.

He walked along the ridge above the jetty. The water vista was utterly serene and calm, without a hint of the chaos that had occurred over the past four days. In the distance were low-flying birds that looked like cormorants, perhaps some of those that had escaped their masters. In this area, fishermen traditionally trained cormorants to fish, tying strings around the birds' necks so they couldn't swallow large fish. The birds would fly back to the fishermen so they could remove the catches from their bills. While fishermen have discontinued the practice, some tour companies continue to train the birds. Mas preferred to think of the cormorants liberated, no master in sight.

He returned to the bench to see that the sardine tin was empty. He hoped that Haruo had been the one to enjoy the treat. It would truly be *zannen* if the sardine instead helped to fortify a rat or another carrier of disease or sickness.

The cooler weather had brought out more mosquitos. After slapping them away from his bare ankles and forearms, he decided to seek refuge back inside.

It was in the middle of night, pitch black, when Mas heard a commotion down the hallway. Another sundowner incident, he figured, but he couldn't ignore the noise, so he slid open his door.

"The American, I need to see the American," he heard a young, high-pitched voice say.

Mas trudged down the corridor toward the front office. Again, he'd forgotten his slippers, and his soles felt cold against the linoleum floor.

When he reached the lobby, he saw it was the village boy with the sad eyes who had been calling out. "Hurry," he said, rushing over to Mas and practically knocking him over. "I think something bad is going to happen to Sora's mama."

Tatsuo came out from the front office, the keys for the company car in his hands. "Let's go."

Sticking his bare feet into some plastic slippers at the *genkan*, Mas realized that he was still in his pajamas. *Shikataganai*. That was the least of his worries.

They got into the car, the boy in the passenger seat next to Tatsuo. "The shore, not far from the A-bomb garden," he said.

What the hell was going on? Mas's heart pounded. Neither Tatsuo nor he asked any questions. They both knew that whatever it was, it was serious.

"Here, here!" the boy called out, and Tatsuo parked the car on the side of the road. They were on a hill overlooking the ocean, the oyster farm barely visible at high tide. There was a full moon, and its light reflected off the water, rippling and undulating.

Mas saw something round and almost luminescent, halfway to the oyster farm. The boy pointed to it, and Mas knew it before he said, "That's her."

Tatsuo was the first to rush over and jump in, followed by Mas. The boy hesitated, as if he were afraid of the sea.

The water was cold, but in the midnight warmth, it felt

more bracing than shocking. Where was Rei? Something brushed his leg and he jumped up in response, almost taking a tumble in the water.

Tatsuo had already reached Rei and she moved—she was alive! Then she was resisting his help, thrashing like a caught animal. Mas knew such fighting was dangerous, not only for the victim but also the rescuer.

Mas yelled in English, "Stop. Stoppu!" His voice seemed to carry throughout the whole bay. Obeying the command, Rei slowly ceased struggling in Tatsuo's hands. She closed her eyes tight and gulped in air.

Tatsuo steered her into shallower waters, and when her feet hit the ground, she focused on Mas. "Arai-*san*. Arai-*san*. You are too old to be in here."

"Then help me," he said in Japanese. She placed her arm around his shoulders and the three of them walked to the shore.

As soon as she was out of the water, she collapsed on a bed of sharp rocks. She didn't react to the pain of that surface and again, like on the tatami at the home, she curled up in a fetal position.

Mas was losing his breath. Putting his hands on his thighs, he bent down. "Where's the boy?" he panted. Tatsuo pointed toward the car and walked over there to retrieve a blanket from the trunk. He wrapped the blanket around Rei, forcing her to stand up. Her teeth were chattering, and her face looked ghostlike underneath the moon. Dripping with water, her hair was clumped together like the fur of a wet white poodle. She looked pitiful, but then they all did. "She needs to be in a warm bath," Tatsuo said, "as soon as possible."

Mas nodded, still trying to catch his breath. Before following them to the car, he noticed something shiny between two rocks and picked it up. A cell phone, one of those newfangled ones. Most likely Rei's, he figured, and he placed it in his shirt pocket.

As the boy was already in the front passenger seat, Mas and Rei rode in the back. There were hardly any streetlights, and Mas's stomach lurched as Tatsuo sped along the curves of the island.

When they arrived at the home, Mas and Tatsuo practically carried Rei into the building and set her into a wheelchair. Luckily, one of the night workers was a middle-aged woman who lived on the island and she took over Rei's care without asking any questions. "After her bath, put her in Room 129," Tatsuo told her, and she nodded.

Tatsuo was still soaked from the seawater, while Mas was wet from the waist down. The boy was out of the car, retrieving his bicycle, which was lying by the road.

Tatsuo stopped the boy before he could ride off. "You can't be riding by yourself in the middle of night. I'll drive you home."

"But my bike . . ."

As the bicycle was too large for the trunk, Tatsuo attempted to stuff it into the back seat at various angles. During these attempts, Mas heard a familiar mewing—*nyaa nyaa*—around his ankles. Haruo had reappeared and was sniffing the brackish, fishy saltwater on the bottom of his pajamas.

"*Kora!*" Mas picked the cat up by the scruff of his neck. *Where have you been?*

"Aaaaah—" The boy came beside Mas and began scratching the cat's chin. "Is this the same one that hangs out at the *torii*? What's wrong with his eye?"

"Probably lost it in a fight."

The boy lifted up his open palms, and Mas deposited the cat into his scrawny arms. "This is Haruo," he said.

The boy scrunched up his nose. "That's a strange name."

When they were all back in the car, Tatsuo engaged the boy in conversation. "What was your name again?"

"Chiba Kenta."

Tatsuo apparently knew the boys' parents. "Do they know that you are out?"

"I told them I was staying overnight at my neighbor's house." The boy cradled Haruo, while the frame of his bicycle bounced against his shoulder. He must have been uncomfortable in that position but he didn't complain. "I was trying to find Sora's mother."

"Why?" Mas asked. "And why come to me?"

"I've seen you walking the island with her. You seem like friends. I hope you won't tell them where I was, will you?"

Neither Tatsuo nor Mas replied. The rest of the ride was dead silent, aside from occasional purring from the cat.

They eventually turned down a narrow alley, the same one that Mas had walked through, and parked in front of a two-story house that was separated from the street by a cinderblock wall. Mas got out of the car to help pull the bicycle from the back seat but stayed back as Tatsuo and Kenta approached the front door.

"What's going on?" Mas heard a woman say. "Kenta, I thought you were doing a sleepover next door." Mas figured she was probably the mother. Another silhouette, a large man, joined the woman in the doorway.

Kenta mumbled something, which failed to satisfy either parent. "Kenta-*kun*, speak up," said the father. "Where have you been all this time?" His voice was booming.

"He actually saved the life of a woman," Tatsuo said.

"Heeeeh." The parents responded with both incredulity and pride.

"Yes, the mother of the boy who was found in the bay."

"Oh, the crazy one who disrupted today's ceremony?" the father said.

"She was trying to commit suicide by the oyster farm," Tatsuo said.

"What were you thinking, Kenta? And what dirty animal are you holding?" The mother was less impressed with her son's actions once she learned who he rescued.

"Isn't that the blind cat that hangs out by the shrine?" the father asked. "It's probably diseased." He tried to wrestle Haruo out of Kenta's arms, and Mas finally walked forward to take the cat.

"Oh my goodness. Kenta-*kun*, go upstairs and take a bath. Take your pants off at the *genkan*," the mother said. After he disappeared in the house, she turned back to Tatsuo before excusing herself. "He hasn't been himself ever since that boy was found."

The father bowed. "Thank you so much for bringing him home," he said to Tatsuo. "We are indebted to you." He said nothing about being indebted to Mas.

Tatsuo and Mas began to walk to the car, but the father called out, "Hey, American." Mas turned around. "The police warned us about you. Stay away from my boy. He has enough problems as it is."

Even though Mas knew the criticism was baseless, it still stung. He recalled all those times as a child when his teachers complained about his behavior. He was the bad Arai, the troublemaker, the brat, the *yogore*. His brothers and sisters, both older and younger, were quiet and respectable. Mas didn't know what happened with him. It was as if all the vinegar and brashness just stayed in the center of the line of siblings, to be manifested in him, the problem middle child. Ironically, this problem child was the last left standing.

The heaviness of these feelings weighed Mas down.

"The boy's father was probably a little in shock." Tatsuo tried to soften the man's accusation when they were back on the road.

Mas kept his eyes on the full moon. The tide had risen in the bay, and now the oyster racks were completely covered.

After Tatsuo parked the car, Mas deposited Haruo on the ground and watched the cat scamper away into the bushes before he and Tatsuo reentered the nursing home. Mas didn't quite understand the shifts of the workers, and Tatsuo explained that there was an extra room connected to the office where he slept after work hours on the island.

"A strange life," Mas commented without thinking,

and Tatsuo nodded. "You can't be a regular person with this kind of life. You are always out of step with the real world."

"Where is the room that Rei is staying in?" Mas asked.

Tatsuo hesitated before answering. "Maybe it would be good for her to just rest tonight." *Message received*, Mas thought. *Stay away from her.*

They bowed their goodnights. Mas moved his packed suitcase to make room for his futon. He couldn't leave as early as he had planned. He had to at least wait until he knew what was going to happen with Rei.

While Mas was undressing in his room, he came across the cell phone he'd found on the shore. He should have turned it in to Tatsuo, but with all the excitement, he'd forgotten. The phone wouldn't turn on, despite his attempts to press and manipulate all of its various buttons. It was a new phone, shiny and sleek, with a case depicting a female character with bare *chichis*. He had assumed the phone was Rei's, but now he doubted it based on the case's image. Anyone who had lost such a fancy, expensive device would be missing it.

Chapter Eight

He was swimming. One moment the world was on fire, and the next he was in liquid darkness. He leapt off the bridge, following his classmate Kenji, who now had polka dots on his skin. *Have you become a cheetah?* Mas wanted to ask him. *Or maybe a ladybug?* Silly Kenji, where had he escaped to? There had been the four of them, Kenji, Riki, Joji, and Mas. But now there was only Mas.

Something hit his shoulder as he swam. And then his stomach. It was solid, like the log from a tree. How did these trees end up in the water? Mas extended his arms to see if he could figure out what was underwater in this blackness. He grabbed hold of a hand. *Hello, hello! I am a Hiroshima boy.* The hand was attached to an arm, but that was all. He realized that he was in a sea of heads, legs, arms, and bodies, all dismembered, cut off from their humanity.

When he awoke, Mas didn't know if he'd been crying out for help, but he thought he'd probably been talking in his sleep. Drool was dripping from his nearly toothless mouth, and a pool of saliva was underneath his cheek, soaking the fitted sheet of the futon. Usually Genessee would have woken him up by now. Enduring his nightmares was a spousal hazard that both Genessee and Chizuko had had to navigate.

He crawled over to the sink, cleaned his face, and stuffed his dentures into his mouth. His watch had fallen off his wrist, so he didn't know what time it was. Judging from the intense light at the edges of the opaque curtains, it must be close to high noon. He finished off a bottle of green tea that he'd left on the counter and got dressed in a fresh pair of jeans and the cleanest shirt in his suitcase. Leaving his room to find Rei, he returned a few seconds later. He remembered something he had forgotten and stuffed it into his back pocket before resuming his search.

Since the room numbers seemed to be organized almost haphazardly, it took Mas a little while to find where Rei was staying. Finally, oddly enough on the second floor, he found Room 129. She was hooked up to an IV machine and staring out the window. She had a view of the ocean, which wasn't a good thing. If he pulled the cord to close the blinds on the window, he could eliminate this scene in real time, but probably not in the girl's mind.

"Hallo."

"*Ohayo*, Arai-*san*."

They stared at each other in silence for a moment.

"You looking better. You have color in your face now."

Rei's blond hair was a tangled mess, but somehow it seemed to suit her more than the smooth bob.

"I'm feeling much better. But then I always feel better when the sun is out."

Mas sat in the chair beside the bed.

"I feel like I've been on this island for years," she said.

Mas did, too.

"I wonder if they felt that. The *hibakusha* who came for refuge. Did they believe they were going to die here, or did they really think they had a chance to survive?"

"They believed they were going to live. The closer you are to death, the more you want to live."

"You sound like you know the feeling."

"I was in Hiroshima when the Bomb fell."

"But you are an American."

Mas frowned. Had he even mentioned that to her?

"I saw the tags on your suitcase. And also your passport." Rei dipped her head down. "I am so sorry. It was wrong of me to spy on you like that while you were sleeping. But you seemed different to me, even that first day I met you. You are like the grandfather I always wished I had."

Rei explained that she was from Hiroshima and most of her older relatives had died either during or shortly after the Bomb. Their fingernails grew like mini elephant tusks, their hair fell out, their skin become spotted. Babies were born with abnormally large heads and died soon after. Since the whole city had experienced the Bomb, the stories were not squashed or silenced; instead, the citizens raised their voices like a chorus. Back in America, such stories were swept into corners, known to the intellectually curious but hidden from people who wanted to believe in fairy-tale endings.

"You're right about people wanting to live," she said. "I was going to do it. I was going to walk into that ocean like Sora did, my brave little boy. But I couldn't do it. However much I hate to be in this world, I'm scared to leave it."

Mas clasped his hands together. His dark hands, callused and strong from decades of gardening, had lost some of their heft; his skin had become loose and pliable over his bones, like gloves that were too big.

"Do you wonder where I was that night?" Rei asked. "The night that Sora walked into the ocean?"

The detective had said something, but Mas had tried not to think about it. Through the slats of the blinds, he saw a colony of seagulls flying. He hadn't seen seagulls until today and it made him homesick for California.

Rei pressed the button to readjust her bed. Apparently, she was serious about her confession and wanted to look at Mas, eye to eye. "I was at a love hotel. I went with my boss. I had asked him for a raise, anything that would help us stay in our apartment."

She swallowed and Mas helped her reach for a plastic cup with a straw. "Sora was beside himself about the move. He would have to share a room with a seven-year-old in my cousin's house." She took a long sip of whatever was in her cup. "He wouldn't be able to hide anymore. He would have to interact with people. I told him it would be a good thing for him, in the long run. But he didn't believe me."

She ran her hand through her nest of hair, making it look even more like it was caught in a tornado. "At the love hotel, I couldn't do anything with him. I locked myself in the bathroom and stayed there all night. Before my boss left he told me through the door that I shouldn't bother to come back to work. I made everything worse. I went there for more money and ended up losing my job."

Oogoto, Mas thought. This was bad news. Without any income, how could the girl support herself?

"I've failed in everything I've touched. Wife, mother to my son. I've even failed at killing myself. What is left to do?" She said all this without shedding a tear. She recited the list of failures like she was a cashier at a grocery store. Her lack of emotion worried Mas. She had given up on life but was still resigned to living.

"You need to tell police," he said.

She tightened her jaw and looked back out the window.

"My friend always talks to me about counseling. Maybe you should look into it." Mas couldn't believe what he was saying, but he was obviously grasping for straws.

"Is your friend Japanese?"

"Well, more or less. Like me. A Kibei Nisei. And a *hibakusha*." Mas pushed himself forward in his chair. "He says that it helps him with his problems."

"Really."

"It works for him."

Mas didn't mention that his friend, Haruo, was dead and now lost in Hiroshima.

"Is that so?" she said, sucking in her cheeks.

Not knowing what more to say, Mas pulled out the cell phone. "Here, I think this is yours. I found it last night."

Rei wrinkled her forehead and fingered the phone. "That's

not mine. It looks like Hideki's. Where did you find it?"

Mas didn't want to say. He muttered something unintelligible and stuffed the device back in his pocket. If this was Hideki's phone, that meant he had been back on the island recently. And if he was, what was he doing here?

After telling Rei to continue resting and regain her strength, Mas headed north for Senbazuru. The phone now felt awkward and obtrusive in his pocket. He needed to get rid of it. He needed someone to look into the phone and find out exactly what Hideki had been up to these last few days.

It wasn't hard to locate Toshi. In spite of the humidity and heat, he was on the baseball field with a full team of boys and one or two girls. He was on the pitcher's mound with two of the players and he seemed to be teaching them catcher signals to indicate the style of pitch—fastball, curve, slider, changeup. He was dressed more casually, in T-shirt and jeans, and occasionally he pulled out a long towel from his pocket to mop up the sweat on his face.

Mas couldn't quite figure out whether or not he could trust Toshi. He'd been friendly enough at their first meeting, but even that had been strange. A dead boy, his best friend's son, was lying on the jetty, and he could still exchange niceties. And then at the hostess bar, his countenance and attitude completely changed. His relationship with Thea was also a cause for concern. She was probably fifteen years his junior, only twenty, a few years older than the oldest children at his school. In some ways, Thea, being in Japan on her own, was mature beyond her years. In Mas's eyes, though, she was still a kid, motivated by passion instead of reason. Had Toshi taken advantage of her?

Toshi walked over to home plate and squatted down like a catcher, flashing signals by his thigh. He instructed one of the boys to take his position and nodded approvingly when the signals matched his intention.

As he waited in the hot sun for the practice to finish, Mas was thankful that he had brought a cold bottle of water that he'd purchased from the vending machine at the home. It was now empty and to ease his tension, Mas had twisted the clear plastic into something unrecognizable. But at last, the practice was over and Toshi sent the children back to some far buildings—perhaps dormitories—and then waved at Mas.

"Arai-*san*, how long have you been here?" After a few pleasantries, Toshi and Mas took the short walk to the director's home. Toshi opened the door, abandoned his tennis shoes at the *genkan*, and went straight to the controls for the air conditioner. He even turned on a stationary fan. This time Mas also took off his shoes.

Toshi brought a large container of barley tea with two glasses to the kitchen table. Mas didn't think he'd ever drunk so much liquid during an entire week while he was in the US.

"So, you will be leaving Japan today," said Toshi, who had obviously heard the news from Thea, an *oshaberi* who apparently needed to unload information as soon as she had received it.

"Actually, there has been a change," Mas said, enjoying the coolness from the fan.

"Oh, really?" Toshi's voice sounded tentative. Was there a tinge of disappointment?

As Mas explained what had transpired the previous night, Toshi reached for his cigarettes. He barely exhaled the smoke. It was as if he was saving it all up inside himself before releasing it.

"She is at the home now," Mas said.

Toshi finally let out a stream of smoke, which dissipated quickly with the force of the fan. Mas let the smoke bathe his face, remembering the joys of smoking, the smooth cigarette in his fingers, and the comforting burn in his throat and lungs. He'd given it up for his grandson and didn't regret it. But it was nice to be around it from time to time.

"What she said to me: 'boy killer.'" Toshi rubbed a spot on his table. "It wasn't about Sora."

Mas waited.

"It was about something else. She wanted to hurt me, especially in front of Thea. And yes, she knew about us. She saw us one time coming out of Hideki's apartment. In some ways, Hiroshima is a small town." The educator's voice was growing fainter and fainter. Mas pulled at his good ear to catch all of his words. "It's about why I was sent to Senbazuru in the first place. It involves my younger brother."

The revolutions of the fan seemed to take over the room.

"It was accident. It wasn't intentional. We lived on the fifth floor of an apartment building in Hiroshima. There were three of us, and I was the oldest at eight years of age.

My mother told me that I was to set an example. Of course, I didn't. She told me to never stand and play around near the edge of the balcony, but I was always jumping off, pretending that I was a Power Ranger. I was supposed to watch my younger brothers, but instead I was jumping. Ryo-*kun* was just doing what I was doing."

Whirl, whirl, whirl. Mas didn't know where to look, so he stared at the spot on the table, too.

"He was only four years old. I'll never forget. . . ." Toshi was as still as a statue. "My mother never completely recovered. And I don't think I did, either. Caused so much havoc in the family that my parents had no choice but to send me away.

"When I saw Sora's body—and I didn't know it was him—I hadn't seen him in so long, aside from the photos that Hideki used to show me. Anyway, when I saw his body on the jetty, I just started thinking of Ryo-*kun*. I felt that part of me had left the island. The only person left was Ikeda the teacher, the director of Senbazuru. It was as if I had separated myself from my past. I had left myself somehow.

"That's why Hideki is so important to me. We grew up here together, and he's like my brother. I want him to eventually move back to the island. I've been telling him that I can find him work fixing people's homes in the village. That would have given me time to work with Sora-*chan*. But Rei. It was Rei who opposed it. She said Ino was no place for a child. It probably didn't help that Sora-*chan* had a bad experience here back in May. Not sure exactly what happened because I was in Tokyo visiting friends. But Rei blames that whole thing on me. Just because I had found a holiday job for Hideki here.

"I don't think Rei was giving enough credit to Sora-*chan*. I've seen the children of Senbazuru survive the death of their parents, abuse, neglect. There are scars, for sure, but they have the strength to continue on. But for adults, it's not so easy. Maybe that's why I like to work with children. They still have a future."

Mas listened carefully as Toshi spoke. He pulled out the phone from his back pocket. "Is this Hideki's?"

"Where did you find this?" Toshi turned over the phone to examine its back cover. "Hideki misplaced this a few days ago. He thought it was lost forever. He just got it this year and it was expensive." He also pushed a few buttons, but nothing.

"The beach. By the oysters."

"But that's impossible. He wasn't anywhere close to the island this past week."

Mas said nothing, but his silence communicated his doubts.

"The night that Sora went missing, Hideki was at a party in Hiroshima. His friends saw him there and even posted photos on Instagram."

"Small boats, here and there," Mas said, implying that Hideki could have taken a private vessel. "Who owns that jetty, anyhow?"

"The owner of an oyster factory. During the summer, he stays in Hiroshima. But it would be impossible for Hideki to come over to Ino on his own in a boat. That doesn't make any sense." Toshi took the phone and plugged it into a cord that was attached to an electrical outlet. "When this charges, we'll find out what was going on."

Mas had no idea how long that would take and took a gulp of the barley tea.

Toshi returned to the table and began drinking the tea, too.

"Where exactly is your family from, anyhow?" Toshi apparently had figured out that Mas's roots were not in the city.

"Kure. Small town over there."

"Aha. By the ocean. Very pretty."

"Haven't gone over there in fifty years."

"Even on this trip?"

Mas shook his head. "What for? Nobody left."

Toshi nodded. "*Sou ne.*" This is true.

After drinking so much tea and water, Mas needed to use the bathroom, which was just across the kitchen. It was a typical Japanese one with only enough space for a fancy high-tech toilet with multiple buttons.

When Mas reentered the kitchen, Toshi was at the sink, washing some dirty dishes.

"By the way, I heard from Thea that you lost Mukai-*san*'s ashes," he said.

Mas frowned as he sat back down. His hunch was right: the girl was an *oshaberi*.

"I bet Mukai-*san* wasn't too happy. She always wants everything her way; she's always getting on my case about my children, but I keep telling her that they are not the ones causing problems."

"She said something like that to me," Mas said.

"But you see, that's not why she's dislikes me. She doesn't like me because I know the truth about her family."

Mas lifted the glass to his lips even though there was hardly any more tea left.

"There was a family scandal involving her brothers starting a construction company. There were bribes to a Hiroshima politician and even a couple of arrests."

"You mean her brothers went to jail?"

Toshi nodded. "It was pretty awful for Mukai-*san*. She's tough, though. She never let anyone know she was suffering. She excelled in school and became a professor. That's commendable, for sure. But no person from a respectable family would marry her. That's how it works in Japan."

"Haruo neva saysu nuttin'," Mas murmured to himself in English.

"Pardon? I didn't hear you."

"Oh, I didn't know," he said in Japanese.

"We have many secrets here." Toshi smiled, revealing his crooked front teeth, a bit discolored from tobacco smoking. "You are peeling back only the top layer."

Something rang—ching-ching; Hideki's phone was now charged. Toshi unplugged it from the cord and pressed a couple of buttons. He poked at it for a few minutes and sighed. "I thought I knew his password but I guess I don't. I may have to wait until I see him. He's supposed to come by today, anyhow."

Mas immediately regretted bringing the phone to Toshi.

He was closer to Hideki than even a blood brother. He would defend Hideki from most anything, Mas figured. But would he even cover up the murder of Sora?

Mas got up from the table. "Don't forget about Sora," he said before he left. "He deserves a friend, too."

As Mas entered the lobby of the nursing home, he heard Tatsuo comment, "That was something else yesterday." He was behind the front desk, organizing some papers.

Mas stopped and nodded.

"That boy keeps coming around. Kenta-*kun*. Wants to see you."

Mas frowned. "His father wouldn't approve."

"I think it's about the cat."

Of course. For some reason, the boy was fixated on Haruo. On his way back to his room, Mas bought a bottle of Coke from the vending machine. He needed a rush of sugar. This wasn't the time for taking naps. It was time to think.

Behind the closed sliding door, he mulled over what Toshi had said. That children were so resilient. He didn't know Sora at all, but from all accounts, the boy didn't come over to the island to die. It seemed like he came to live.

Taking his Coke bottle with him, he went outside and sat underneath the camphor tree. Sweat dripped from his forehead and the soda soon became lukewarm. He saw another giant worm traveling on the hot pavement. He doubted it was the same one he saw the first day he was here.

Just when he was about to return back inside, he heard the spinning of metal. Sure enough, it was Kenta on his bicycle. He got off underneath the camphor tree and used his kickstand to park the bike.

"I made this for the cat," he said and held out a collar fashioned of carefully knotted blue yarn. Hanging from it was a leather tag with the name Haruo in hiragana.

"Ah—" Mas said. "Haven't seen the cat since last night. You made this?"

Kenta nodded.

Mas studied his handiwork, neat and precise. As a fisherman, Kenta's father certainly would be adept at tying knots in working with nets. "You hang onto this for the next time you see Haruo."

Putting the collar in his pocket, the boy sat next to Mas on the bench. The cicada started their chirping and the two of them listened for a while.

"Don't you have any brothers or sisters?" Mas finally asked.

Kenta shook his head.

"You lonely?"

"Only sometimes. I actually like being by myself during the summer break."

"Why do you hang out with those *yogore* boys?"

The boy shrugged his shoulders. "Not too many boys my age around."

As if on cue, the cicada stopped singing, an intermission from their concert in nature. Drops of rain hit the leaves of the camphor tree and dripped onto the pavement, evaporating almost immediately.

Mas suspected that Kenta wasn't here for just the cat. "What happened to Sora? Do you know?"

The boy's eyes grew larger while his mouth seemed to shrink until it was a tiny "O."

"We didn't want anything bad to happen to him." Kenta put his hands in his pocket. "Even Daisuke. We didn't want him to die."

"Who's Daisuke? The fat one?"

"Um, yes."

The boy described their first encounter with Sora during Golden Week, Japan's national weeklong holiday in May. He had come with his father to do repairs on people's homes. "We tried to play with him, but he was strange. Weird. In the end, he was screaming about something. His father was trying to calm him down. I don't know what it was all about."

"He was strange, so you bullied him. Told him to die." *Shi-ne.*

"That wasn't me. I never said that."

"Your friends did. And you didn't stop them."

Kenta's hands tightened into little fists. "We were just playing a game with him that day. After getting off the ferry, we ran into the village to get our bikes. We weren't thinking about Sora until we saw him walking alone toward the east side of the island. Then Daisuke made up a game. We were spies. We were supposed to follow Sora and figure out what he was doing here.

"He saw that we were following him and then he started to run and hide. For not being from the island, he was pretty good. I was the one who spotted him. He had gone into one of those oyster factories that were closed for the summer. The one closest to here."

Mas almost couldn't breathe. Sora had come to an island with a mission.

"Take me to it."

"Why?" Kenta looked afraid, as if wisps of the dead boy's soul might remain in the places he visited had on the last day of his life.

"Let's go."

They went back on the same paved road that Mas had traveled back and forth to Senbazuru. The second oyster factory was a little farther off the path, closer to the water. It stood on stilts on the shore. One side was completely open, revealing a large container full of light-colored scallop shells. The only way to enter was through metal steps connected to the elevated platform.

"Here." Kenta pointed to the platform. "Sora was in there."

"Go on. Show me." Mas gestured that the boy should go up the stairs. He hesitated again. Perhaps he was afraid of heights. Finally Kenta climbed up, with Mas right behind him.

On the platform, beside the container, which was about six feet tall, were an electric fan and low green plastic crates. Mas noticed walls of corrugated metal siding on the east and south side along the shoreline.

"What was he doing in here?" Mas said out loud, more for his own benefit. He repeated the same question to Kenta.

The boy hemmed and hawed. He nervously looked left and right to make sure they were alone. "I saw him searching for something in back of this container. And then he pulled out a green bag. While he was checking the bag's contents, I waved for the others to come over. We all hid underneath the platform, so when Sora climbed down the stairs with the bag, we were waiting for him.

"Daisuke was the one who took it. The bag. Then we all rode away on our bicycles. Sora didn't yell or chase after us, which was no fun. So Daisuke went back and told him that we'd be hiding the bag somewhere on the island and he'd have to find it."

"What was in the bag?" Mas figured that the boys must have looked.

Kenta said he wasn't sure. "But I think it was money."

"What happened to it?"

Kenta shook his head. He didn't know. "Daisuke was the one who had it. Sora was going crazy looking through every spot on the island. The park, the school, the garden. We got tired of watching him and rode our bicycles back home. I guess we all kind of forgot about it that night."

This whole tragedy was a result of a prank? Mas was livid. "Why didn't you tell anyone?"

"We didn't want to get into trouble. Daisuke said we all could be sent to jail for what we did."

Obviously a silly threat to keep the boys' mouths shut. Daisuke being the ringleader, he probably feared that he had the most to lose. Mas turned to leave. He'd had enough.

"It was this kind of bag." Kenta held up a green canvas bag from a stack of folded ones. It wasn't that big, maybe a half a foot. Mas had seen a bag like that somewhere before—the one that Tatsuo had given him with his lunch of rice balls and fried chicken.

Before Mas could respond, they heard the echo of footsteps on the metal stairs. "What are you doing in here? You know this is private property."

Chapter Nine

The Japanese *oni*, or demon, looked a lot like the American devil, Mas realized. It had horns and maniacal eyes, and its skin could be red in color. But in Japan, there wasn't a singular devil, a top dog that bossed the lower ones around. Instead, there were multiple demons who could wreak havoc or, conversely, protect people. Mas and Chizuko, in fact, had kept a demon mask in their hallway to ward off evil spirits. He tried to explain its role to the church going Genessee, but she wasn't having any of it. The *oni* mask was wrapped in newspaper and like many of Mas's possessions after Genessee moved in, stored in the garage. He wasn't about to destroy the mask or throw it away and risk it falling into the hands of the wrong person. He wasn't a superstitious man, but there were lines that even he wasn't willing to cross.

Mas was eye level with Tatsuo, who stood on a lower step of the metal factory stairs. As he looked at Tatsuo's face—the eyes blinking furiously again—the *oni* came to mind. Was Tatsuo one of those Japanese demons who was able to conceal his true identity? Or was he a good one who would scare away evil ones?

"This is no place to play." Tatsuo continued climbing until he reached the platform. He directed his admonishment to Kenta, but Mas knew that he was also supposed to receive the same message.

"This is no playing," Mas said. "It's about Sora."

Tatsuo winced.

"This your uncle's company, right? The one that he owns?"

"You shouldn't have come to Ino. This is not your place." Tatsuo was going on the offensive. A surprise move for the usually passive and taciturn office worker.

Thinking about the green bag, Mas stepped up his game, too. "Why did you leave money for Sora? What had he done to earn it?"

"I don't know anything."

"I betcha don't," Mas muttered in English. And then a lie in Japanese: "The boy saw you. And he saw Sora picking up the package."

Kenta's mouth fell open.

"I don't know a thing," Tatsuo said. "I was just doing it as a favor."

Mas had never heard anything so ridiculous. Who leaves money around for someone in a secret place as a favor? "For who?"

"I can't say. I promised not to say."

"This whole thing has got to stop."

From the water came the chug of an engine. A ferry had

arrived at the landing.

"I think you need to leave, Arai-*san*. I'd recommend that you go on that ferry right now. We can send over your luggage straight to the airport."

Another cover-up. Mas was tired. He wasn't going to play nice anymore. A long, sharp hook on a pole leaned against the corrugated aluminum siding. He had no idea what the tool was used for, but he grabbed it and waved it in front of Tatsuo's blinking right eye.

"You like your eye, don't you? Don't lie. Why did you give a bag of money to Sora?" In his anger, the Japanese tumbled out of him, an awkward cling-clang of words. His heart was beating so fast. Maybe he had the guts to poke out Tatsuo's eye.

"Have you gone *kuru-kuru-pa*?" But Tatsuo stood still, his eyes on the sharp hook that was inches from his face.

"Tie his hands with that rope over there," Mas commanded Kenta. The boy quickly did his elder's bidding, fashioning an impressive restraint around the nursing-home worker's wrists.

"You're going to regret this," Tatsuo sputtered.

"*Yakamashii!*" Mas yelled at him to shut up and shook the hook closer to his face. "Kenta-*kun*, the rag on the floor, stuff it in his mouth."

The boy stood motionless, his hands hanging limp by his sides.

"Kenta!"

He gingerly picked up the dirty rag and began to poke it in the man's mouth.

Tatsuo spat it out. "There's old fish scales and grease on that thing."

Oh well, Mas thought, perhaps that was going overboard. He told Kenta to forget about it and instead go to the landing to see if Sora's father had arrived. "You know what he looks like?"

Kenta nodded.

"Okay. Then go over to the boat and bring him back here."

"What should I tell him?"

"Tell him it's about Sora. And if he's not on the boat, go over and get Ikeda-*sensei* from Senbazuru."

Kenta bit his lip in determination. Bam, bam, bam, his footsteps clanged on the metal stairs on his way down.

His hands bound together, Tatsuo wasn't putting up a fight. He was certainly angry, however. Mas could feel his bitterness. "You don't understand," said Tatsuo. "None of it." But he offered no explanation.

After about ten minutes, Mas heard a series of footsteps on the stairs. It was Toshi and Hideki, with Kenta following behind.

"What's this all about?" Toshi was dressed in a button-down shirt, his collar wide open.

"Sora came to this factory after he arrived on the ferry. This guy, Tatsuo, left money for him here."

"Is this true?" Hideki asked. Toshi, meanwhile, gestured for Mas to lower the hook.

"I don't know anything. I just did what was I told."

"By who?"

"Tell us, Tatsuo-*san*."

Tatsuo sunk down to his knees, his hands still secured. "Gohata-*san*."

Toshi seemed skeptical. "Why would Gohata-*san* leave money for Sora?"

"I didn't know who was coming for it. Gohata-*san* told me to do it. He was off the island and said that it needed to get done that day. I didn't ask questions."

Hideki had become strangely quiet. In fact, he'd taken a few steps back toward the stairs.

"Wait a minute. He knows something." Mas began waving the hook again, this time in the direction of Hideki.

"Stop with that," Toshi said. "Hide-*kun*, what is going on?"

Hideki's face took on that mask-like quality again.

"How could he be involved?" Toshi said to Mas. "He had nothing to do with Gohata."

Hideki, who'd failed to immediately defend himself, finally spoke up. "I did actually have some dealings with Gohata."

"You don't even know him."

"I saw them talking in the village before." Kenta piped up. They'd all forgotten that the boy was even there.

"I don't understand. I really don't. He couldn't have known anything." Toshi kept shaking his head. "What trouble have you gotten in now?"

Again, Hideki wasn't talking.

"What's the passcode for your phone?" Toshi held up the phone with the risqué manga cover.

"Where did you get that?"

"Tell me."

Hideki recited four numbers, which Toshi punched in. The principal turned his back on the setting sun and looked through the phone, his fingers moving rapidly on the screen.

"What? What's on my phone?"

"Who is 'Majin'? Is that your name for Gohata?"

Hideki's face grew red.

"That's from Dragon Ball Z," Kenta said. Mas figured that was some kind of game. "Majin Boo is a demon."

Toshi handed the phone over to Hideki, who scrolled through it. "I didn't write those messages."

"I know. I know how you text and those last messages don't seem like yours. Sora must have taken your phone and assumed your identity. He became you in these text messages with Gohata."

Hideki stared at the screen in disbelief. "He was demanding 200,000 yen." The sum astounded him. "I don't understand. You mean that he came over to get money, but for what purpose?"

Mas felt heat rush to his head. "Because he didn't want to move away." The apartment manager had mentioned that Sora's mother owed him 200,000 yen.

"Rei never told me that she needed money."

Toshi crossed his arms and hugged his chest.

"What?" Hideki asked his friend.

"Let's be real, Hide-*kun*. If she told you, what could you have done?"

"Maybe rob a *konbini*. Break into one of those nice

houses by Hijiyama Park."

"That's probably why she didn't want to tell you."

"Now you sound like Rei." Hideki stuffed his phone into his pocket. "So someone killed Sora over the money he had received?"

That part was unclear to Mas.

"You mean my boy risked his life for this? To stay in that hellhole of an apartment?"

"It was his home. Only place he could relax," Mas said.

Another other thing had not been answered. What did Hideki have on Gohata? It was obvious that Sora hadn't come up with this blackmail scheme on his own. Hideki must have extorted the district representative before.

"Is someone going to untie me?" Tatsuo asked from the floor.

Both Kenta and Toshi went to his aid. Toshi was carrying a penknife and used it to saw through the rope.

"I did the knots," Kenta shyly told Toshi.

"You're certainly good at it." Toshi grinned. "What's your name?"

"Chiba Kenta."

"Kenta-*kun*, do you play baseball? You should play with us sometime."

Tatsuo's hands were loosened and he got to his feet and rubbed his left wrist with his right hand.

"I'll be calling the police," Toshi said. "I wouldn't tell anyone else about this, okay, Tatsuo-*san*?"

Tatsuo glared at each one of them. He saved his most venomous look for Mas. "After all I did for you.

Baka American," he said and disappeared down the steps.

Tatsuo's slur stung. Mas was surprised that it did, because he'd been called a lot worse in California over the years. Tatsuo had been invaluable during his tumultuous trip to the island, and Mas felt awful to return that hospitality with threats. The voiceless Sora needed an advocate, however, and that superseded any cultural codes of contact. Mas was not Japanese, after all.

He, Toshi, and Hideki all gathered around the kitchen table at Senbazuru. Toshi was making coffee in an espresso maker over the stove. He served it black and strong in small cups. This would be a long night.

"So, tell us," Toshi said to his friend.

Hideki began. That first morning during Golden Week, he had been feeling good. He and Sora were on the ferry together. It had taken quite a bit of cajoling to get Sora to cooperate, but here they were. "He liked it. He liked the seawater hitting his face. The ferry moving along the water." Tears welled up in Hideki's eyes. "I told him that water was magic. That he shouldn't be afraid of it."

Then they went from house to house in the village— doing odd jobs. Fixing a leaky toilet. Repairing a lock. Weatherproofing a door. "It was like we were a regular father and son," he said. "It was amazing."

Everything changed when they went by Gohata's house to move stones in the garden. "An old lady comes out of the house. She's carrying something in a box. She tells us that it needs to be buried. Put to rest. I have no idea what she's talking about." Hideki gulped down the rest of his coffee, which must have been lukewarm by then. "Sora opens it. It's a skeleton."

Mas felt like a force was pressing against his chest.

"A skeleton of a baby. The skull almost didn't look human. It was too large for the body. It looked like an alien. The old lady says that's her baby." So the pregnant Kondo-*Obasan* in her daughter's story had given birth. How long had the baby been alive?

"Sora is screaming. I finally am able to calm him down. The old lady has disappeared. I decide that I need to take Sora back to Hiroshima." Hideki's body seemed too stiff, as if he was still holding something back.

Toshi suspected there was more, too. "And what else?" he prodded.

"I took the bones back to Hiroshima with me."

Toshi started cursing. "How could you do such a thing?"

"I lost my mind. I don't know. But I thought this might be an opportunity."

Toshi kept shaking his head. "I don't believe this. I just don't believe it."

"I had Gohata-*san*'s phone number, so I call it. I tell him what I have and we meet in downtown Hiroshima. He tells me if I give him back the bones and keep my mouth shut, he will give me 100,000 yen."

"What were those bones from and why would you take money for them?" Toshi practically spat in disgust. "And why is it such a secret?"

"He never told me."

"And I'm sure you just threw that money away."

"From that first time, that's how I was able to go to San Francisco to visit my friend. I've always wanted to go there and ride the cable cars. I wanted to take Sora with me, but I didn't have enough money for him. And, of course, he was too scared to leave his room.

"I told my friend in San Francisco that I'm going to get serious and make some money. So that Sora can see this someday."

"You said 'first time.' How many other times did you ask for money?"

Hideki's narrow shoulders slumped forward. "One other. A month ago. But that was for only 50,000."

"Evidence of all of that is on your phone," Toshi said.

"I'll need to get rid of those texts." Hideki pulled out his cell, only to have his friend grab it away.

"You are not going to get rid of anything. This all has to go to the police."

"Toshi-*kun!*" Hideki looked shocked that his friend was going to sell him out.

"Do you want to find out what really happened to Sora? I mean really?"

Hideki clenched his teeth. "Of course."

"Well, then, we need to come clean with everything."

Hideki's silence signaled acquiescence.

Toshi pressed on the phone's screen. "There's this last text on the phone. It's from some other blocked number, telling Sora to go to the oyster factory at sundown."

"Gohata?"

"I'm not sure. I mean, who else had your number?"

"Just you. And of course, Rei."

"Since the atomic-bomb commemoration in Hiroshima is tomorrow, I'm not sure if I'll be able to reach Suzuki-*san*, but I'll at least leave a message on his cell." Toshi went outside to make his phone call.

Hideki reached for a crumpled pack of cigarettes on the table only to discover that it was empty. He patted down his pockets. Empty as well. He sighed. "I've been an awful father. I know that."

Mas placed his palms over his coffee cup, as if he were trapping a small bird. "We've all fallen short. Me, too." Only Mas had had a second chance with his daughter. There would be no opportunities of redemption between Hideki and his son.

Toshi came back inside. "He didn't answer," he said from the *genkan*. "Get your shoes on. It's time for a little conversation with Gohata-*san*."

They took Senbazuru's vehicle, a small white van used for special excursions. Toshi was a skilled driver who anticipated the turns of the road in spite of the darkness. There were hardly any street lights, because why would there be a need for them? Normally, no one would be driving to the village at this hour. Luckily, the moon, which had been full a few days ago, was still bright.

Toshi navigated the narrow roads with ease. He drove the van as far as it could go and parked against a wall. "We'll have to walk from here."

All the lights inside the *konbini*, aside from the ones in the refrigerated case, were off. Toshi grabbed a flashlight from a compartment on the driver's-side door. As a steward of vulnerable children, he seemed always prepared. Although Mas had previously taken this elevated path to the district representative's house, at night it seemed unfamiliar.

When they reached the porch, Toshi pounded on the door. The house was dead quiet. A string of small lights had been hung around the garden, the only bit of whimsy that Mas had witnessed in the village. "At least the sister-in-law should be home," Toshi muttered, pounding again.

Hideki seemed distracted by the garden. "We did all of this work," he said, pointing to the broken pieces of stone that formed the walkway. Mas was thoroughly unimpressed. In his professional gardening heyday, he could have created that walkway with his eyes closed and even then, it would have resulted in something more artful.

"There's no one here. Maybe there's a meeting at the community center."

They walked down the pathway, Toshi's flashlight swinging back and forth with each downhill step. When they reached the van, something moved by its front bumper. Mas at first thought it could be a large animal, but as Toshi aimed his flashlight toward it, they saw it was a boy, the chubby ringleader, Daisuke. He seemed to be making his getaway.

"Wait. Daisuke, isn't that your name?" Toshi called out.
The boy froze.

"Why are you running away from us?" Hideki asked.

"No reason." He crossed his fleshy arms. He was young,
yet he already had a double chin.

The three of them surrounded the boy. He showed no
fear, a criminal in the making. Toshi aimed his flashlight
right on his forehead.

Mas could not keep silent. "You bullied Sora-*kun*."

"Who says?"

As he couldn't reveal Kenta's identity, Mas paused.

"What did you do with the money?" Toshi took over
the interrogation.

"I don't know what you're talking about."

"Sora's money."

"That wasn't his money."

Daisuke may have been strong of body but he was weak
in mind. Realizing that he had divulged too much, he said,
"You're going to get in trouble for harassing me."

"You're going to get in trouble for killing a boy."

"I didn't kill him."

"What did you do then?"

Hideki inserted himself. "Tell us. Sora was my son."

Daisuke narrowed his eyes in reaction to the force of
the flashlight. "It was just a prank, okay? I took the bag and
was going to hide it. But then I opened the envelope inside.
It was filled with money."

"What did you do with it?" Toshi asked.

"I was counting it on the steps of my house and

Gohata-*san* sees me. Asks me where I got the money and I tell him. He says that he's going to take care of everything."

"And what else?"

"What?"

"How much money did he give you to keep your mouth shut?"

Daisuke's eyes rolled back and forth like one of those old-fashioned American Kit-Cat Clocks. He sighed. "Half of it."

"Do you know where he is?"

Silence.

Toshi, of course, didn't raise a hand against the boy, but Mas could see the anger in his eyes.

The boy blew out air from his cheeks. "He's taking off in his boat."

Toshi gestured to Mas and Hideki and they headed to the van. There were small jetties all around the island, and Gohata's private one wasn't far from the main landing where the Shinto shrine stood. As they took off in the van, it was apparent that Toshi was fueled by adrenaline as he swerved dangerously close to a narrow drainage ditch by the side of the road.

When they pulled up to the jetty, Gohata was untying his boat. Toshi led the pack as they hurried from the van toward the jetty. "Don't you think it's unsafe to take a boat out in the middle of the night?" he said.

Gohata leapt into his boat, pulling a cord to start the engine.

"*Kora*, stop!"

Mas was amazed to see Toshi run to the jetty and jump off into the water.

Something must have been wrong with the motor because it sputtered out. Gohata began to curse and the boat began to rock. Fingers appeared on the starboard side and then a soaked Toshi pulled himself up into the boat. Another splash and Hideki was in the water and also climbing into the boat to help Toshi subdue Gohata, who resisted them as much as he could. He was not a match for the two men who were half his age.

Mas carefully stepped onto the jetty and caught the rope that Toshi tossed to him, easing the boat to the side of the dock. He heard Hideki yelling at Gohata, "How could you do that to my boy? How could you kill him?"

Gohata stepped out of the boat, the two younger men gripping each arm.

"None of you understand," the district representative said. "You are half-breeds. Rejects. Outsiders. My only granddaughter is getting married next year. Into an elite family in Kyoto. They have no stain. They can't tie themselves to a bloodline that may have been marred by the Bomb."

They took Gohata to the Ino community center and found a storage room for which Gohata, ironically, had the key on his keychain. Toshi and Hideki stuffed him in there amid stacks of toilet paper, paper towels, and computer paper. Toshi wrote a sign and affixed it to the locked door:

"CRIMINAL SUSPECT. DO NOT OPEN WITHOUT PERMISSION OF IKEDA TOSHI AT SENBAZURU."

"At least he has plenty of paper to wipe his *oshiri*," Hideki commented as they prepared to leave. Even Mas had to smile at the rude remark.

On the drive back, Hideki began to cry. It was a few tears at first, but then full-on sobs, his body convulsing.

"Don't throw up in the van," was Toshi's only response. Mas noticed that he was gripping the steering wheel hard with both hands, even though their path was completely straight.

Toshi stopped in front of the nursing home. Mas could see the light of the office through the glass door. Tatsuo was probably in there.

"I don't think I can go back there," Mas said, remaining in the back seat.

Toshi turned and grunted. "True. It'll be a bit crowded, but stay with me. We can pick up your suitcase tomorrow."

As they got closer to Senbazuru, Toshi rolled down his window and sniffed. Mas smelled it, too. Fire.

Hideki had stopped crying and sat up. "Smells like smoke."

In front of the building, practically on the concrete street, was a hibachi, glowing with heat. Kneeling beside it was Thea.

Toshi parked the van on the side of road. "What are

you doing?" he asked.

"Ah, Mas is here." Thea's voice was light and cheery, a welcome contrast to what had occurred that night. "I think I have a solution to your problem." She noticed that both Toshi and Hideki were completely drenched. "What happened to you two?"

"We'll explain. Let us get out of these wet clothes and take a shower first." They both went into the house while Mas stayed back with Thea.

She was obviously excited about something. "Look what I made, Mas." She brought out a metal canister that had once held green tea leaves. Inside was not tea but something that resembled brown dirt, only finer, with hard, white bits mixed in.

"Look like ash," Mas said.

Thea gave him a toothy grin. "*Yatta!* I made it out of ground-up shells and a concoction of other things. Kind of broke Toshi's coffee grinder, but I can get him another. Worth it, though, right? I cooked everything in this fire. You can now take this to Mukai-*san* and tell her this is her brother."

The girl's ingenuity caught Mas off guard. He had underestimated her.

"Whatchu doin' with dis fire now?"

"Aha, another surprise." She picked up some tongs that she had placed on a newspaper and removed something wrapped in aluminum foil from the hibachi's grill. Letting it cool a little on the newspaper, she nestled it into a towel and presented it to Mas.

"Watch out, it's hot."

He picked at the foil.

"Ah, sweet potato," Mas said.

"Kind of," she said. "I guess there's not enough light to really see. Look." She brought out her phone and fiddled with a setting so that a beam of light focused on the tuber. Snapping the top of it, she broke the skin.

"*Murasaki*," Mas noted the color.

"Yes, purple. I saw these at the store, and it reminded me of the yams from my country. They are called *ube* over there."

"Okinawa have same kind of thing," Mas remembered.

"You know about Okinawa?"

"My wife born there," he explained. As soon as he said that, he needed to hear Genessee's voice that very second. It was an imposition to use Thea's phone for an international call, but she didn't mind. "I call my sister all the time in the States. She lives in Kentucky." Mas was constantly amazed at the young woman, that her world could be so expansive.

"Hello."

"Hallo."

"Mas! Oh, Mari's here. She's wanting to talk to you, hang on."

After a few seconds, Mari's voice came through the phone. "Dad, Shoko-*san's* been calling. She wants to make sure that you come by."

"Yah, yah."

"Don't yah, yah me. You don't know whether you'll ever

be in Hiroshima again. This may be your last opportunity to see the family house."

She returned the phone to Genessee. "Are you all right? Your voice sounds hoarse. I hope you're not overdoing it."

"No," Mas told her. "Takin' it easy."

Chapter Ten

Mas remembered traveling on the same train line—not the same train car, of course—when he was about nine. His older brothers got fitted for custom-made suits for a family portrait, but time had gotten away from his mother, and they had to leave before Mas was measured. Again, he was passed over and he couldn't stand it. He made a fuss from the tailor's to the Hiroshima train station and then on the rail car. His older brothers were sick of it and they weren't the only ones. "Go over there and sit down," his mother, clothed in a kimono, commanded. He was mad as hell and refused to sit among strangers in the back. The anger shot up to his head and there was no containing it. He rushed to the open side door and jumped.

He didn't know how he survived the fall and neither did anyone else who witnessed it. He had rolled close to the bottom of the track but only sustained a bruised knee.

"You're *baka*," his brothers had said to him, but were incredulous over his luck. From then on they said, "*un ga ii*," that Mas, the middle child, was blessed with good fortune.

He thought that was a terrible joke, one more way that they twisted the knife in his back.

The rail car going toward Kure was vacant. The Hiroshima train station itself had been crowded, with both Japanese and gaijin in town for the atomic-bomb commemoration. By the time Mas reached the port of Ujina on the ferry, the morning ceremony was over. The whole town seemed festive, with an air of electricity. *All fools*, thought Mas, *as am I.*

Who would think about going home after all these years? It was ridiculous. Meaningless. Real home was Altadena, California, the place where he became a father, had two wives (not at the same time, of course), and helped raise a grandchild. California was open and free, with purple mountains and salty brown-water beaches and dying palm trees and lavender jacaranda trees. Liberated green parrots found refuge in California, squawking as loud as they could on power lines in the early morning hours. Coyotes roamed the streets at night during the occasional downpour. Brown bears bathed in swimming pools and mountain lions stalked hiking trails. It was a magical place where anything was possible. That was home.

But as the train car bounced and click-clacked over rail ties, Mas realized that what was outside these windows was also home. The graceful arches of the Japanese roofs and color of the foliage on the hills—not *midori*, American green, but *ao,* the word used for blue but also a blue-green. The name of the color of the sky could not be separated from the color of the trees here in Japan.

There was also the sense of *shibui*, the love for negative space, to keep the canvas of life a bit empty to allow something unexpected to permeate it. And the turns of the Japanese garden, how to open up the world by taking a stroll in a different direction. As much as his head and heart tried to reject Japan, his body felt that this was home, too.

He prepared for the next stop, his destination. He had no idea if his niece, Shoko, would be waiting for him at the station. She was overcome with anticipation when he told her over Thea's cell phone that he planned on stopping by. Mas was a little bewildered. They didn't know each other and her mother had only been ten when he left Hiroshima. She might have been at his and Chizuko's wedding reception in Hiroshima; he honestly didn't remember.

The station was nothing to look at—back then and even now. Only one stationmaster was manning the ticket gate and he'd probably just entered his twenties. It was an old, sleepy station with none of the polish and commerce of the Hiroshima one. Mas was the only passenger to debark here and he stopped in the restroom, a dirty, stinky hole of a place that the stationmaster was obviously neglecting.

There was no one in the waiting room and Mas poked his head out to see if anyone was outside. Instead of open fields, the small town was crowded with housing. He could probably somehow find his way to his old house, but he wasn't keen on wandering around through the maze of tiny streets under the hot sun. Then a white car stopped by the side of the station. In the driver's seat was a woman around Mari's age. She waved and smiled and when Mas approached the car, he was startled to see that the woman had the same face and expressions of his little sister.

"*Mah*, I'm so sorry to keep you waiting," she said through her open car window. "Please, hurry, get inside. It's so terribly hot."

Mas got in, carrying a gift of *kaki yokan*, a block of sweet bean mixed with bits of persimmon, that he'd purchased at the train station. Chizuko would always tell him that his sense of Japanese etiquette was terribly lacking, but he knew enough not to come on this visit empty-handed.

Her car was small, with barely room for two people, but perfect for the narrow streets of the old village. Mas couldn't stop staring at his niece. She was a stranger yet so familiar. There was something about her voice that reminded him of his mother.

They headed up a hill and Mas held onto the dashboard to look out the front window. He remembered all these houses, which were far enough from ground zero to be spared. The family home of Joji and Akemi Haneda, also American-born like him. The three of them formed a tight-knit unit during World War II. The Hanedas, more Americanized with a father in the US, were especially suspect and regularly visited by the military police.

Shoko pulled into a neighbor's driveway and backed into a narrow carport that had only enough space for the miniature car. "C'mon, let's go inside. The air-con is on."

Mas slowly opened the door, grasping hold of the gift bag with the other hand. As his feet hit the pavement, he got goose bumps. His body remembered.

He was greeted first by a rock frog statue next to a "poodled" pine, its greenery carefully manicured into pom-pom shapes. *Ohayo, Mr. Matsu*, he silently addressed the pruned tree. It had to be the same one. "Hey, you'zu older than me," he couldn't help commenting out loud.

"What?" his niece asked, amused.

"You've taken good care of this place," he said, returning to speaking Japanese.

The door and window frames seemed to be of the original wood. Mas was amazed. With the heat and humidity of the region, it was difficult to control mildew and mold. Mas and his niece left their shoes at the *genkan*, and walked down a narrow hallway that had windows overlooking the garden.

Mas truly didn't know why they had that garden. It wasn't like every household had one. But somehow his father, a rice farmer, had felt one was necessary to make his mark in this world. Mas saw more pruned pines, floating orbs of green clouds. And a bunch of hedges cut into domes like the heads of mushroom children. The pond, which had once held goldfish and koi, was bone dry. Too much of an expense to maintain, Shoko explained. She opened up a wooden sliding door and ushered Mas into the traditional Japanese tatami room.

He knew the configuration of this area with his eyes closed. First there was a small section where the Buddhist altar, the Butsudan, stood from the floor straight to the ceiling. It was gold and ornate, with a lithe standing figure of Buddha at its center. Mas didn't understand why Buddhas came in all shapes and sizes, with some roly-poly and gregarious, others solid, serene, and regal. This one was dainty, almost feminine. As he walked past, he was assaulted by the brief but pungent smell of incense.

Beyond the Butsudan was a rectangular area with windows, perhaps six mats in size. Like most other tatami rooms, a wooden trim adorned the walls about a couple of feet from the top. Above the trim over the entryway were framed black-and-white photographs of Mas's parents, the soft face of his mother and the stern, distant visage of his father.

In their movements from Japan to America and back to Japan, their lives had been hectic and rootless. Too many mouths to feed, too many tragedies to overcome. Mas knew that a sibling had died in childbirth between him and his next older brother. Maybe that's why he felt like an afterthought during most of his youth. Perhaps the sadness of a child dying had enveloped his mother, clouding her body not with hope but with fear, leading to a sense of disconnection.

Friends like Joji became his lifeblood. And Haruo, too. With friends, he could choose. More often than not, they chose him. He had no idea why the best of the best, sweetest of the sweet, were drawn to him. Opposites attract—he was well acquainted with that saying. Either way, he always seemed to end up on the winning end.

"Please sit on this." Shoko brought out a padded back rest that he could use to sit against. He bowed and settled in on the floor in front of a low table as she rushed out and returned with a platter of sliced melon and cantaloupe, along with a bunch of giant grapes. Mas knew enough about exorbitant produce prices to realize that this offering had cost her a small fortune.

"Ah, here," he said as he handed over the confection, embarrassed that it came from Hiroshima rather than California.

"You didn't have to do that."

She apologized for the absence of her husband, who'd gone into Hiroshima for the atomic-bomb commemoration. They had lived in the city before his mandatory retirement from his company at age sixty. Mas was surprised that the Japanese were forced out of full-time employment at such a young age. For himself, sixty was when he was just starting to hit his stride.

Shoko and her husband had moved into the family house in the Kure countryside after her mother had passed away. No one else seemed open to taking care of the house. "Too bad that she didn't see you before she died."

Mas grunted, not really understanding what his niece was getting at.

"She spoke of you from time to time."

Mas was confused. Shoko's mother was the runt of the family, the little one who was always getting underfoot. Mas didn't remember saying more than two words to her as a teenager.

"She always said that you were the exceptional one, the trailblazer."

More like the black sheep that had wandered off, Mas thought.

"To go to America on a boat by yourself at age eighteen, nineteen. That's unthinkable." She peeled one of the giant grapes with her fingers before popping it into her mouth. "From there, you were able to move to Rosu. Get a house. Start a family."

Why did she know so much about his life? He'd never shared anything much with his family in Hiroshima once he left.

She reached for a small photo album in the middle of the table and flipped it open. "Chizuko-*san* would send letters and photographs to the house. My mother was the one who assembled them in a photo album. See."

On the first page was a family portrait captured on the day he left to take the boat to the US. It was taken in the garden here in the house. This time, he had a suit to wear, as did his older brothers. His younger brother was about twelve, while Shoko's mother, the only woman in the photo as Mas's elder sister was already married and living away, wore a dress with some kind of pattern, maybe flowers. Mas recalled that day, a day of excitement and adventure. His mother had cried a little; her eyes were wet. He wasn't thinking of goodbyes; he was thinking of hellos to California and distant relatives there. If he knew that this was the last time he would see his parents and his siblings, at least before he returned briefly to get married, his thoughts would not have raced to the unknown future, but stayed here in this garden.

He turned to the next page and the next. There were photos of him as a young man in Watsonville—his hair cut and styled in a James Dean pompadour. Underneath that photo, someone, presumably his little sister, had written *onisan*, big brother, in hiragana. *Onisan, onisan, onisan* was written all throughout the photo album. Mas couldn't remember ever hearing someone address him with that title, but the words on the page seemed to have a voice.

There were other photos, including his wedding portrait with Chizuko. He was dressed in a rented tuxedo and she in the traditional Japanese kimono, her face powdered white. And then pictures from Altadena, California: Mari as a baby, then a surly teenager with the mouth full of metal braces, later wearing a cap and gown as she graduated from high school. In the background was the house on McNally Street, the autumn leaves of the neighboring sycamore trees carpeting the grass. The parade of images ended around the mid-1980s.

"They were all proud of you. No one wanted to take a chance to go to America after Papa and Mama couldn't make it themselves. Too much discrimination. But you took a chance and went back. And you made something out of yourself."

At this point, Mas had to interject. "No, nothing like that. I'm just an ordinary man."

"Don't be so humble. It's just like when the Bomb fell. You were the only one in the city. Everyone thought you were dead. I heard the stories. My mother, though, wasn't surprised. She said that '*un ga ii.*'"

Mas sat at the table with the small photo album in a state of disbelief. How could he be considered one of the lucky ones?

On the other hand, how could he not?

Mas was in a daze as he traveled back to the island. In his eighty-six years of life, he'd pictured himself as a lone wolf, but maybe this whole time he wasn't so alone. He didn't know what to do with that information.

He was now comfortable enough with present-day Hiroshima that he could navigate through the train station without giving it much thought. He walked down the stairs of the building and waited in line for a taxi to go back to the Ujina Port.

"It's hot, isn't it?" the gloved taxi driver said from the driver's seat.

Mas, who was sitting in the plastic-covered back seat, only grunted in response.

"So busy with all these tourists today. And tonight with the *toro-nagashi* down the Motoyasu River, all the young people will go out. It's like a party. Nothing really about peace." Mas had seen footage on the NHK channel of the colorful paper lanterns being released on the water. The way the news depicted the festival was solemn and purposeful. Leave it to the masses to make it about something else.

"I tell my children and grandchildren to go the night before. When it's quiet and you can really memorialize the dead. If that's what you're after."

After the journey by train, taxi, and ferry, when Mas

finally got to Toshi's house, he was exhausted. Since Toshi didn't lock his front door, Mas walked right in. The empty house was warm and the faint scent of coffee remained in the kitchen.

On the kitchen table was a sealed plastic bag filled with brown powder. It was identified with a Hello Kitty Post-it as "Ashes for Mas." He picked it up and grinned.

She had gone to all that trouble. The effort should not be wasted.

Thankfully, after he walked from Toshi's house and into the nursing home, the younger man, Makoto, was manning the front office. As he bowed to Mas, he probably hadn't heard about what happened.

She was in a wheelchair facing the window. Before he could say anything, she said, "I saw you walking up the road."

"Ah, Mukai-*san*," Mas gave his apology in Japanese. "I am so incredibly sorry about everything."

"Yes, yes." She turned her wheelchair with both hands. Her arms were still strong, judging from the force she used to turn herself toward him. Ayako's eyes, however, looked strange, sickly. They were yellowish, and the surface was a bit milky. It was as if her eyes were melting.

"It's not going to be long," she said and they both knew that she was talking about her death.

"Dis is Haruo. Dis is your brotha." He presented the bag with both hands, his palms up with the bag of ashes resting on top. He bowed as low as he could manage.

To his astonishment, Ayako snatched the bag from

him, as if it was filled with gold dust.

"I knew it. You were hiding his ashes all this time. To watch me suffer." Her hands wrapped around the bag, practically strangling it.

Ayako seemed unhinged and Mas became worried about her state of mind.

"You cared about my brother."

Mas nodded. *My best friend.* He didn't say that out loud.

"His wife said that you were like his brother. That you were the only person she trusted to bring over the ashes."

He thought it was because he was the only one available.

"Let me ask you this. What kind of person do you think my brother was?"

What a question. "Nice guy."

Ayako cackled, a string of spit shooting out of her mouth onto her cotton robe. "Is that the best you can say about your 'brother'?"

Her sarcasm was not lost on Mas. This was not a good look on her.

"Let me tell you some things about Haruo Mukai. He was lazy and a simpleton, unaware of how half-human he looked with that ugly scar on his face. Because of that scar and missing eye, everyone felt sorry for him. He didn't have to lift a finger because someone would appear to take care of all of his needs. What did he do instead? Pursue fun. Gamble away the little money he had. He was certainly not a 'nice guy.' "

Mas was well aware of Haruo's gambling addiction, which had followed him from Japan to the US. His

weakness had led to one broken marriage, but he reformed
himself through counseling.

"When my older brothers got into some trouble, who
was there to take care of it? Oh, not Haruo. He had fled to
America. My younger sisters were married with families of
their own. No, it was up to me, the *nesan*, to handle it. I had
to rely on my brains, my know-how, to dig us out of pov-
erty and rebuild our good name. I was able to go to college
and get my doctorate. Become a professor to support us."
Ayako put her wrinkled hands over the bag of ashes on her
lap. "And now I'm left here, on this island of an island, to
spend my last days."

She coughed, first a rasp and then a series of hacks that
caused her whole body to shake.

"Youzu orai? I getsu someone to help out."

"No, no, no!" Ayako was insistent. She flailed her arms
for emphasis. "Take me to the bathroom."

Mas grimaced. The absolute last thing he wanted to do
was take an old lady into the *benjo*.

"Do it!" she ordered. *Shikataganai*. After everything
that had happened on this trip, this wasn't a big deal, he
told himself.

He wheeled Ayako into the private bathroom. The
toilet was low with metal grab bars installed on the wall.
Mas was beyond embarrassed and stood there helplessly.
But Ayako didn't move from the wheelchair.

"You never forget this. You watch this and tell Haruo's
wife, children, and grandchildren where he ended up here
in Japan." With that, her bent fingers clawed through the

plastic and she released the ash of island shells into the toilet and flushed.

After her angry display, Ayako was satisfied. She brushed her hands of any remaining ash and rolled herself out of the bathroom and back into the main room. She returned to her original place by the window, her back to Mas.

"You may go now," she said.

Mas nodded. He was only too happy to.

As he returned to the hallway, he felt weak in the knees. Haruo, the gentle, harmless Haruo, was viewed by his older sister as a pariah, a user. The Haruo she knew and distorted in her mind was not the same Haruo who had matured and grown old in America.

Mas stumbled to the vending machine in the cafeteria, this time pressing the button for an iced coffee. Caffeine and sugar could perhaps jolt his heart into beating again. The cafeteria was empty and he sat down to get the coffee in his system.

He was halfway through his drink when the last people he wanted to see entered the room: Kiseki Kondo and her mother, Kondo-*Obasan* the thief. Kiseki wasn't wearing her trademark scarf or head covering. Her short hair was snowy white and almost feathery like the back of an egret. Instead of a walker, Kondo-*Obasan* was using the bend of her daughter's elbow to help her shuffle forward.

He was making his getaway when Kiseki said, "Ah,

Arai-*san*. May we join you?"

Mas was shocked, to say the least. He was, after all, the man who'd helped lock up her brother-in-law.

Kondo-*Obasan* settled in a seat at the end of the table as her daughter returned with a tray of three cups of steaming hot tea.

They sat for a while in silence as they sipped their green tea. Kondo-*Obasan* did not make eye contact and she seemed more interested in the way the sun was hitting the windows.

"I saw my brother-in-law this morning," Kiseki said.

"Yah?" Mas was tongue-tied. Was Gohata set loose or still in the storage room of the community center?

"He admitted it all to me," she said. "He's promised to report it all to the police tomorrow."

"Oh."

"I guess Toshi-*san* has appointed himself the new district representative. And jailer. My brother-in-law has returned to our house but Toshi won't leave his side. I guess we now have a boarder." The wrinkles on Kiseki's leathered face were deep. The vertical lines between her eyebrows made her look like she was perpetually frowning.

"He shouldn't have done that. Not to that poor boy. But Bunpei lost his head. He was doing it for the family's sake. For his granddaughter's. For me and for his wife, my sister."

Mas refused to excuse Gohata for any reasons of filial piety.

"He didn't mean to raise a hand against the boy. He just wanted to warn him not to say anything to anybody. But the boy wouldn't listen. He said that he was tired of being pushed around and no one could tell him what to do."

"So Gohata hit him with his walking stick."

Kiseki widened her eyes. "How did you know? Did you see it?"

Mas shook his head. He had figured that for the detective to return to the island, a new cause of death had been determined. It wasn't accidental drowning. And when he heard that Gohata had met Sora under the cover of night by the oyster farm, he knew there must have been an altercation. Gohata had said he practiced kendo for years. A master kendoist would know where to strike his opponent. It was second nature.

"But for your sake? And your sister's?" Mas still didn't understand that reasoning.

"Whatever you may think of Bunpei, he's a good man. He married my sister Yoko, knowing about our family's history. There weren't many like him back then. And then Yoko was struck down by a mysterious sickness, causing people to wonder if it was connected to the Bomb. Then news came about my grandniece's possible engagement. We all felt the pressure to stamp out any rumors that our blood may be tainted."

Hiring investigators to look into one's family lineage for an impending marital union used to be commonplace in Japan, especially during Mas's youth. But to hear that it was still taking place was a surprise.

"Here, Mama, drink." Kiseki held the handleless Japanese cup to Kondo-*Obasan*'s chapped lips. She took a few slurps before nodding her head that it was enough.

"I was going to be married once," Kiseki said, wiping a few drops of tea from her mother's blouse. "A long time ago. Bunpei was the go-between. But then people were talking about our eldest sister."

The one whose bones had been stored in some secret location.

"She was born damaged. Broken. Because of the Bomb. Who would have known how long she would have lived?"

"How did she die?" Mas had to ask. He had his suspicions, but he wanted an answer, whether it be the truth or a lie.

Kiseki's face transformed into its usual hardness. She wasn't going to talk. As her mother started to murmur something, Kiseki rose and helped her to her feet.

"We have to go. I just wanted you to know that my brother-in-law is not a bad man."

Mas bowed. That, of course, was a matter of opinion. Gohata may have had good intentions, but they didn't erase the fact that a boy was dead.

He went back to his room, the clashing combination of the sweet coffee and bitter green tea remaining in his mouth. After making sure that his airline ticket to go home was still in a zipped compartment in his suitcase, he lay down on his futon, thinking that it was quite fortuitous that he was to leave on a red-eye flight the next evening. It was certainly time to go home.

Someone rattled his door. He slid it open to reveal Tatsuo, who got right to the point. "I believe that this may be what you were missing." He produced the bag of Haruo's ashes tied together with green gardening twine.

"Where—"

"Because today was the sixth, I went to the memorial outside to do some cleaning. I found the ashes placed in between two markers. Based on the dust and dirt on the plastic, it must have been there the whole time."

Mas was stunned. Kondo-*Obasan* must have figured out what the bag contained and left it in the most appropriate place.

"We have a locked safe at the bottom of the memorial for ashes. Do you want me to keep them in there?"

Mas shook his head. He wasn't sure where they should be left, but here wasn't the place. "How is Rei-*san*, by the way?"

"A social worker has come to talk with her. She'll need other people to help her through this. She'll be released tomorrow."

Mas grunted. He was grateful that Rei would not be alone.

"I didn't know what Gohata-*san* did. To the boy. I would never have left the money in the factory if I knew what was going to happen."

Mas believed him. Tatsuo was one of these straight-arrow types who did well in a world that was black and white. Unfortunately reality was rarely that way. "I'm sorry that I caused all sorts of problems for you," said Mas. "Everything I did back at the oyster factory. I know you were just doing as you were told." He did feel bad that he had considered Tatsuo a bit of an *oni* when he was actually more of a guardian angel.

"I said things that I regret," Tatsuo said, referring to when he called Mas a stupid American.

"I am *baka*. At times."

With the addition of "at times," they both laughed. *More times than not* was a better answer. But that much latitude was allowed between friends.

Chapter Eleven

When Mas slid open the door to his room at the nursing home, he discovered a gift that had been left for him. It was blue-green, actually the color of his old Ford truck, and had four working wheels in excellent condition. A brand-new suitcase, compliments of Thea.

She had left him a handwritten note. She dotted her 'i's with hearts; Mas had never received a letter with so many hearts on the page. In his mind, he wished the girl well. She was actually quite extraordinary to tackle a new country, especially a closed one like Japan, by herself at her age.

He dumped out everything from his broken-down bag. Tatsuo had allowed him to use the home's washer and his garments were all dry—albeit a bit stiff—after being on hangers for one night. He stuffed his clean clothing into his new suitcase. Just that simple act energized him.

Leaving his packed suitcase in his room, he went into the cafeteria and served himself some *okayu*. He knew that he must be starting to lose his mind on the island, because the rice gruel tasted okay. When he was half finished, the cafeteria worker came to his table with her personal stash of *kobu* squares. Twisting open the jar, she offered it to Mas.

"We've made a deal," she said through her paper mask. "I'll bring the food and he has to come regularly to feed it."

"Huh?" Mas struggled to understand her abrupt announcement.

"The boy. Kenta. I saw him this morning looking for the cat. He even brought an old pickle container to serve as a dish. I'll have some table scraps and pet food to feed it."

"*Domo arigato.*" Mas bowed his head a couple of times.

His flight was not due to leave Kansai Airport until midnight. He had promised Rei to accompany her on the ferry to Ujina. Then he had several hours to be *bura-bura* before boarding the bullet train to the airport.

While he sipped his green tea, one of the workers placed a second bowl of *okayu* on his table. Before he could respond, Kondo-*Obasan* sat in the seat across from him.

"*Musume* is asleep now," she said, spooning up some gruel. *Musume* was daughter in Japanese, and Mas had a feeling that she wasn't talking about about either Kiseki or Yoko.

Mas picked up a few seaweed squares with his chopsticks and popped them in his mouth. He chewed them thoroughly and swallowed. He watched as Kondo-*Obasan* struggled with her spoon. It took a couple of tries, but she finally got it into her mouth.

In the light of day, she seemed to have a new lease on life. Mas could even make out a pair of pupils underneath her flaps of skin. Would she be ready to talk?

"What happen to *musume-chan*?" he asked, as if they were longtime friends.

"Ah, *musume*. That was something else, wasn't it?"

"Unn, unn." Even though he had no idea what she was talking about, he wanted to encourage her to keep going.

"They took her to take a bath. And then she didn't come back," Kondo-*Obasan* reported, bits of gruel stuck on the sides of her lips. "But I found her and hid her so they wouldn't take her again."

"Who gave her a bath?"

"My husband," she said. "He took care of everything."

Mas figured that someone in the family had ended the deformed daughter's life, and now based on what he just heard, it could have been the baby's own father. It was such a sad business, with no easy answers. How would Mas have dealt with a brain-damaged child who might be in pain and suffering? Through the window, he could see that someone had strung loops of origami cranes next to the Buddha statue.

"Don't cry," Kondo-*Obasan* said. "She's fast asleep now."

Mas rolled his new suitcase down the corridor and met Rei in the lobby of the nursing home. Her hair had been freshly washed and blown dry into the same smooth bob she'd had when he first met her. She was skinnier now and had bags underneath her eyes, but she gave him a quick smile.

"Ready?" he asked.

"Ready," she responded.

Instead of her handbag, she carried a plastic bag. They stepped on a mat in front of the glass doors, causing them to whoosh open, and then were surrounded by the heat and *tsuku-tsuku* chirps of the cicadas. Mas picked up Rei's umbrella, which hadn't been moved from the original spot where he'd left it.

They reached the ferry landing in the nick of time. The boat had already anchored, with the portly captain collecting yen coins.

As Mas walked onto the boat, he wondered if he would miss Ino Island. This trip to Hiroshima had changed the course of his life, or at least what was left of it—whether it was several more years, months, weeks, or only days. It was making him reconsider everything and everyone, including his fellow Kibei Nisei like Joji and Akemi Haneda, Riki Kimura and, of course, Haruo. For the first time, he regretted that he never had a chance to spend time with his siblings as adults. Even at eighty-six, how much did he not understand about himself and his family?

He also wondered about Rei. She was leaving the place where her son had died, but would soon be arriving in the city where he had lived. Which was easier to deal with? At least she wouldn't be spending time alone in the same apartment. She was headed for her cousin's place outside of Hiroshima. Maybe the country air and the wildflowers would lift her spirits.

They sat outside on the deck, salt water misting their faces.

"Maybe you move out of Hiroshima?" Mas asked.

"No, I only know Hiroshima. Not many can leave and make it."

"I haven't made it," Mas said.

"You raised a daughter. Have a new wife. Maybe I'll find a new husband when I'm seventy years old."

To hear Rei make a joke encouraged him. And she spoke about getting older, which was the most optimistic goal she could commit to right now.

While the boat powered toward the city of Hiroshima, they watched the green mound of Ino Island become smaller and smaller until it was a simple green triangle, merging into the sky and the sea.

Before they reached Ujina, Rei turned to Mas. "Oh, and I saw a social worker. She told me about that counseling you were talking about." She lowered her voice as if she was afraid that another passenger would hear. "She gave me a name of someone in Hiroshima. I'm thinking of going."

Mas almost had to laugh. He didn't know how Haruo was able to do it, even reduced to mere ashes sitting in his suitcase. When Haruo was alive, he constantly poked and prodded Mas to consider telling a professional about his problems. Although Mas refused to heed this advice, he had somehow become his dead friend's messenger.

As the boat docked, a woman about Rei's age stood on the landing, grasping the long handles of a handbag with both hands. A boy and a girl ran circles around the woman; their mischievous behavior signaled that they were related.

The woman waved to Rei, who raised her hand in acknowledgment and then bowed from the boat. This must be the cousin, and she had children. Would they remind Rei about what she had lost? Or perhaps they could be the repository for Rei's love, which currently had no home.

Mas didn't like emotional, public goodbyes and made sure that he said his sayonara on the deck of the boat. "Take care of yourself," he said to her, standing and bowing.

"I hope we keep in touch," she replied, her eyes shiny with tears.

Mas grunted. "Yah," he said but he knew they wouldn't. He probably would never hear from her again.

Mas was first in line for a taxi and was surprised to see that it was the same driver he'd had earlier.

The driver also recognized him. "*A-ra*, again," he said, rushing out of his black cab to place Mas's suitcase into the trunk.

When Mas told him that his destination was Hiroshima police headquarters, the driver made a peculiar expression, but it was fleeting. He was a professional after all.

"Oh, it's been hot, huh?" he said, driving up the boulevard. He'd been busy these past couple of days, he told Mas. So many gaijin from dozens of different countries. He'd probably driven to the Peace Park or the Peace Dome a hundred times over the past forty-eight hours. And the releasing of lanterns turned out to be as crowded as he predicted. Visitors waited an hour just to let their handwritten messages go down the Motoyasu River.

"Many of the gaijin were very moved," the driver told Mas. Many had mentioned Sadako, the young girl who'd died from radiation sickness a decade after surviving the Bomb. While bedridden, she had taken to folding origami cranes from red medicine papers. She aimed for a thousand, the number that ensured a long life. She didn't make it, but then her friends joined in. This simple act of kindness had led to the folding of billions of paper cranes by people all around the world.

Mas had seen photographs and video footage of the skeletal remains of the Atomic Bomb Dome, the building that miraculously survived the blast, and of the Sadako monument, her arms stretched out, holding a giant origami crane above her head. All of these memorials had been either preserved or produced after his time. They were for future generations, the ones who hadn't experienced what could happen in a split second. Giant waves and the shaking of the ground could still destroy cities, but that was at the hands of Mother Nature. It was entirely different when the engine of destruction was human— different because it was calculated and planned for reasons both good and evil. But when that power was unleashed, who would it touch? It touched them all—the highest of the high and the lowest of the low. And even more frightening, it sent out a sickness that polluted your body, mind, and soul, and maybe also the generations to come.

They drove along the Kyobashi River, which was flanked by outdoor cafés and restaurants with colorful umbrellas. After a few minutes of traveling into a more residential area not far from Thea's assisted-care facility, the driver finally stopped in front of a mid-size building. Made out of metal, Hiroshima Police Headquarters had rows of windows that were either frosted or too dirty to see into.

"We have arrived," the driver said.

At the reception desk, Mas made his request to see Detective Suzuki. After the detective was informed of his presence, Mas and his suitcase were placed in a small conference room. Within a few minutes, the walls seemed to press in, making it difficult for Mas to breathe. He was almost ready to leave when the conference room's door opened, revealing Detective Suzuki with his hedgehog hair.

"Ah, Arai-*san*."

Mas cut right to the chase. "I want to let you know I'm leaving Hiroshima today."

"Thank you for letting me know."

They stared at each other for a moment.

"Is there anything else?" the detective asked.

For a moment, Mas felt like a fool. Hadn't Suzuki instructed him to keep him abreast of his date of departure?

Mas shook his head. That task completed, he set out for the lobby when Suzuki announced, "We are expecting Gohata-*san* to come in today."

Mas was surprised and waited to hear more, but the detective offered only that. Gohata would most likely be confessing to killing Sora. Would he be accompanied by Toshi Ikeda?

"Ikeda-*san* told me what happened. Also that you were key in figuring it out."

Two young people wearing paper masks entered the lobby and headed for the reception desk.

"Too bad you aren't younger, Arai-*san*," Suzuki said before Mas left the building. "Hiroshima could sure use you as a detective."

As his new suitcase had dependable wheels, Mas leaned on the extended handle as he walked. *Hiroshima could sure use you as a detective.* Suzuki's statement hit him squarely in the gut. There was a trace of respect in his joke.

Clouds had gathered, providing a respite from the blazing sun. The sky looked like it would break out in rain soon. Mas needed to make a decision quickly.

From the police station, he proceeded a few blocks to the place he'd been a few days earlier, Shukkei-en Garden. A group of seniors—bonnets on the women and white golf caps on the men—waited by the entrance, offering docent-led tours of the grounds. Mas, of course, declined their invitation. He knew the general direction of where he wanted to go.

He walked toward the river, where the stone memorializing the souls of the dead was placed. He remembered seeing something in this general area. And there, he found it.

It was a Buddha in a low-standing display box, barely visible through a grid. Interpretive signage in both Japanese and English explained that the wooden Buddha had survived a flood in the area two hundred years ago. This one and two others came floating down the Kyobashi River to the garden and then were housed in a special altar within the property. Then came the Bomb and the destruction of the two larger Buddhas. But this smaller one, a couple of feet high, survived.

Mas placed his face right next to the grid of the box so he could clearly see this Buddha's bulging eyes and prominent nose. The statue's mouth was half open, as if he were protesting his situation.

"Youzu survived flood and *pikadon*, atomic blast," Mas declared to the Buddha.

This had to be as good a place as any. He opened up his new suitcase and took out the bag of ashes. Removing the gardening twine from the bag, he sprinkled some of Haruo around the altar, so that visitors looking for the Buddha would also get a whiff of his friend. He then went to the riverbank, which was cordoned off from the garden by a three-foot fence.

A strong breeze kicked up, blowing through the pine branches.

Mas bowed for a moment and then raised the open bag high toward the river, finally setting the ashes free.

THE END

Acknowledgments

Research for *Hiroshima Boy* was made possible through a grant from the Aurora Foundation in Los Angeles. My relatives in Hiroshima also aided me in getting a sense of the historic Ninoshima, the island that is the model for Ino.

I thank Prospect Park Books and its founder/leader, Colleen Dunn Bates, for continuing the Mas Arai series to this final novel. Amy Inouye, Dorie Bailey, Caitlin Ek, Jean Barrett, Sherry Kanzer, and Margery L. Schwartz all contributed to make this release of *Hiroshima Boy* as special as possible. Props go to readers who contributed character names for this novel: Carrie Morita, Chris Mason, Emily MacInnis, Cynthia Hughes, Pat Shiono, and Kathy Kumagai. And, of course, my creative "team," which includes agent Allison Cohen of Gersh and my husband and fellow traveler, Wes Fukuchi.

About the Author

Naomi Hirahara is the Edgar Award–winning author of the Mas Arai mystery series. Nominated for the Macavity and Anthony awards, the series includes *Sayonara Slam, Strawberry Yellow, Blood Hina, Snakeskin Shamisen, Gasa-Gasa Girl,* and *Summer of the Big Bachi.* She is also the author of the Ellie Rush mystery series, as well as *1001 Cranes,* a novel for children. A graduate of Stanford University, Naomi has also written many nonfiction books about gardening and Japanese American history and culture. Learn more at naomihirahara.com.